THE EARTH BOOK
OF STORMGATE

Three

THE EARTH BOOK
OF STORMGATE
Three

Poul Anderson

NEW ENGLISH LIBRARY/TIMES MIRROR

To Geoff Kidd

First published in the USA in 1978 by Berkley Publishing Corporation

First NEL Paperback Edition February 1981

NEL Books are published by
New English Library Limited,
Barnard's Inn, Holborn,
London EC1N 2JR.

Made and printed in Great Britain by
Hunt Barnard Printing Ltd.,
Aylesbury, Bucks.

0 450 04926 4

ACKNOWLEDGEMENTS

These stories were originally published as follows:
'A Little Knowledge', *Analog Science Fiction/Science Fact*, August 1971. Copyright © 1971 by Condé Nast Publications, Inc.
'Day of Burning' (as 'Supernova'), *Analog Science Fiction/Science Fact*, January 1967. Copyright © 1967 by Condé Nast Publications, Inc.
'Lodestar', in *Astounding: John W. Campbell Memorial Anthology*, ed. Harry Harrison, Random House, 1973. Copyright © 1973 by Random House, Inc.
'Wingless' (as 'Wingless on Avalon'), *Children of Infinity*, Roger Elwood, ed., Franklin Watts, 1973. Copyright © 1973 by Franklin Watts, Inc.
'Rescue on Avalon', *Boys' Life*, July 1973; Copyright © 1973 by The Boy Scouts of America.

A CHRONOLOGY OF TECHNIC CIVILIZATION

Note: Although Poul Anderson was consulted during the preparation of this chart, he is not responsible for its dating nor in any way specifically committed to it. Stories are listed by their most recently published titles.

21st C   century of recovery.

22nd C   interstellar exploration, the Breakup, formation of Commonwealth.

2150   'Wings of Victory,' *Analog Science Fiction* (cited as ASF), April, 1972.

23rd C   establishment of Polesotechnic League.

24th C   'The Problem of Pain,' *Fantasy and Science Fiction* (cited as F & SF), February, 1973.

2376   Nicholas van Rijn born.

2400   Council of Hiawatha.

2406   David Falkayn born.

2416   'Margin of Profit,' ASF, September, 1956 (van Rijn).

             'How to Be Ethnic in One Easy Lesson,' in *Future Quest*, ed. Roger Elwood, Avon Books, 1974.

———   'Three-Cornered Wheel,' ASF, October, 1963 (Falkayn).

stories overlap around	'A Sun Invisible,' ASF, April, 1966 (Falkayn).
2426	*War of the Wing-Men*, Ace Books, 1958 as 'The Man Who Counts,' ASF, February–April, 1958 (van Rijn). See below: *The Earth Book of Stormgate*.
———	'Birthright,' ASF, February, 1970 (van Rijn).
2427	
	'Hiding Place,' ASF, March, 1961 (van Rijn).
	'Territory,' ASF, June, 1963 (van Rijn).
	'The Trouble Twisters,' as 'Trader Team,' ASF, July–August, 1965 (Falkayn).
	The Trouble Twisters (includes 'The Three-Cornered Wheel,' 'A Sun Invisible' and 'The Trouble Twisters'), Berkley Books, 1966.
2433	'Day of Burning,' as 'Supernova,' ASF, January, 1967.
	'The Master Key,' ASF, July, 1964.
	Trader to the Stars, Berkley Books, 1964.
	('Hiding Place'), Berkley Books.
	('Territory'), Berkley Books.
	('The Master Key'), Berkley Books.
2437	*Satan's World*. Doubleday, 1969, and ASF, May–August, 1968; Berkley Books (van Rijn and Falkayn).
	'A Little Knowledge,' ASF, August, 1971.
	'The Season of Forgiveness,' *Boy's Life*, December, 1973.
2446	'Lodestar,' in *Astounding: The John W. Campbell Memorial Anthology*, ed. Harry Harrison, Random House, 1973 (van Rijn and Falkayn).
2456	*Mirkheim*, G. P. Putnam's Sons, 1977 (van Rijn and Falkayn).
late 25th C	settlement of Avalon.
26th C	'Wingless on Avalon,' *Boy's Life*, July, 1973.
	'Rescue on Avalon,' in *Children of Infinity*, ed. Roger

Elwood, Franklin Watts, 1973.

dissolution of Polesotechnic League.

The Earth Book of Stormgate (contains 'Wings of Victory,' 'The Problem of Pain,' 'Margin of Profit,' 'How to Be Ethnic in One Easy Lesson,' 'The Man Who Counts,' 'Birthright,' 'Day of Burning,' 'A Little Knowledge,' 'The Season of Forgiveness,' 'Lodestar,' 'Wingless on Avalon,' 'Rescue on Avalon'), G. P. Putnam's/Berkley, 1978.

27th C   the Time of Troubles.

'The Star Plunderer,' *Planet Stories* (cited as PS), September, 1952.

28th C   foundation of Terran Empire, Principate phase begins.

'Sargasso of Lost Starships,' PS, January, 1952.

29th C   *The People of the Wind*. New American Library and ASF, February–April, 1973.

30th C   the Covenant of Alfzar.

3000   Dominic Flandry born.

3019   *Ensign Flandry*. Chilton, 1966. Abridged version in *Amazing* (cited as Amz), October, 1966.

3021   *A Circus of Hells*. New American Library, 1970 (incorporates 'The White King's War,' *Galaxy* (cited as Gal), October, 1969.

3022   Josip succeeds Georgios as Emperor.

3025   *The Rebel Worlds*. New American Library, 1969.

3027   'Outpost of Empire,' *Gal*, December, 1967 (non-Flandry).

3028   *The Day of Their Return*, Doubleday, 1973 (non-Flandry).

3032   'Tiger by the Tail,' PS, January, 1951.

3033   'Honorable Enemies,' *Future Combined with Science Fiction Stories*, May, 1951.

3035   'The Game of Glory,' *Venture*, March, 1958.

3037   'A Message in Secret,' as *Mayday Orbid*. Ace Books, 1961, from short version, 'A Message in Secret,' *Fantastic*,

December, 1959.

3038	'A Plague of Masters,' *Fantastic*, December, 1960–January, 1961 as *Earthman, Go Home*. Ace Books, 1961.
3040	'A Handful of Stars,' as *We Claim These Stars!* Ace Books, 1959, from abridged version, 'A Handful of Stars,' Amz, June, 1959.
3041	Molitor succeeds Josip as Emperor after brief civil war, supplants short-lived Imperial relative as Emperor.
3042	'Warriors from Nowhere,' as 'Ambassadors of Flesh,' PS, Summer, 1954.
3047	*A Knight of Ghosts and Shadows*. New American Library, 1975 and *IF*, September/October–November/December, 1974.
	/story on Flandry's old age planned/
early 4th millennium	Interregnum.
	Dominate phase.
	Fall of the Terran Empire.
mid-4th millennium	The Long Night.
3600	'A Tragedy of Errors,' *Gal*, February, 1968.
3900	The Night Face. Ace Books, 1978 as *Let the Spacemen Beware!* Ace Books, 1963 from short version 'A Twelvemonth and a Day,' *Fantastic* Universe, January, 1960.
4000	'The Sharing of Flesh,' *Gal*, December, 1968.
7100	'Starfog,' ASF, August, 1967.

As a dewdrop may reflect the glade wherein it lies, even so does the story which follows give a glimpse into some of the troubles which Technic civilization was bringing upon itself, among many others. Ythrians, be not overly proud; only look back, from the heights of time, across Ythrian history, and then forward to the shadow of God across the future.

This tale appears at first glance to have no bearing on the fate-to-be of Avalon. Yet consider: It shows a kindred spirit. Ythri was not the sole world that responded to the challenge which, wittingly or no, humans and starflight had cried. Like the countless tiny influences which, together, draw a hurricane now this way, now that, the actions of more individuals than we can ever know did their work upon history. Also, Paradox and Trillia are not galactically distant from us; they may yet come to be of direct import.

The tale was brought back to Ythri lifetimes ago by the xenologist Fluoch of Mistwood. Arinnian of Stormgate, whose human name is Christopher Holm and who has rendered several Ythrian works into Anglic, prepared this version for the book you behold.

A LITTLE KNOWLEDGE

They found the planet during the first Grand Survey. An expedition to it was organized very soon after the report appeared; for this looked like an impossibility.

It orbited its G9 sun at an average distance of some three astronomical units, thus receiving about one-eighteenth the radiation Earth gets. Under such a condition (and others, e.g., the magnetic field strength which was present) a subjovian ought to have formed; and indeed it had fifteen times the terrestrial mass. But – that mass was concentrated in a solid globe. The atmosphere was only half again as dense as on man's home, and breathable by him.

'Where 'ave h'all the H'atoms gone?' became the standing joke of the research team. Big worlds are supposed to keep enough of their primordial hydrogen and helium to completely dominate the chemistry. Paradox, as it was unofficially christened, did retain some of the latter gas, to a total of eight percent of its air. This posed certain technical problems which had to be solved before anyone dared land. However, land the men must; the puzzle they confronted was so delightfully baffling.

A nearly circular ocean basin suggested an answer which studies of its bottom seemed to confirm. Paradox had begun existence as a fairly standard specimen, complete with four moons. But the largest of these, probably a captured asteroid, had had an eccentric orbit. At last perturbation brought it into the upper atmosphere, which at that time extended beyond Roche's limit. Shock waves, repeated each time one of these ever-deeper grazings was made, blew vast quantities of gas off into space: especially the lighter molecules. Breakup of the moon hastened this process and made it more violent, by presenting more solid surface. Thus at the final crash, most of those meteoroids fell as one body, to form that gigantic astrobleme. Perhaps metallic atoms, thermally ripped free of their ores and splashed as an incandescent fog across half the planet, locked onto the bulk of what hydrogen was left, if any was.

Be that as it may, Paradox now had only a mixture of what had hitherto been comparatively insignificant impurities, carbon dioxide, water vapor, methane, ammonia, and other materials. In short, except for a small amount of helium, it had become rather like the young Earth. It got less heat and light, but greenhouse effect kept most of its water liquid. Life evolved, went into the photosynthesis business, and turned the air into the oxynitrogen common on terrestrials.

The helium had certain interesting biological effects. These were not studied in detail. After all, with the hyperdrive opening endless wonders to them, spacefarers tended to choose the most obviously glamorous. Paradox lay a hundred parsecs from Sol. Thousands upon thousands of worlds were more easily reached; many were more pleasant and less dangerous to walk on. The expedition departed and had no successors.

First it called briefly at a neighboring star, on one of whose planets were intelligent beings that had developed a promising set of civilizations. But, again, quite a few such lay closer to home.

The era of scientific expansion was followed by the era of commercial aggrandizement. Merchant adventurers began to appear in the sector. They ignored Paradox, which had nothing to make a profit on, but investigated the inhabited globe in the nearby system. In the language dominant there at the time, it was called something like Trillia, which thus became its name in League Latin. The speakers of that language were undergoing their equivalent of the First Industrial Revolution, and eager to leap into the modern age.

Unfortunately, they had little to offer that was in demand elsewhere. And even in the spacious terms of the Polesotechnic League, they lived at the far end of a long haul. Their charming arts and crafts made Trillia marginally worth a visit, on those rare occasions when a trader was on such a route that the detour wasn't great. Besides, it was as well to keep an eye on the natives. Lacking the means to buy the important gadgets of Technic society, they had set about developing these for themselves.

Bryce Harker pushed through flowering vines which covered an otherwise doorless entrance. They rustled back into place behind him, smelling like allspice, trapping gold-yellow sunlight in their leaves. That light also slanted through ogive windows in a curving wall, to glow off the grain of the wooden floor. Furniture was sparse: a few stools, a low table bearing an intricately faceted piece of rock crystal. By Trillian standards the ceiling was high; but Harker, who was of average human size, must stoop.

Witweet bounced from an inner room, laid down the book of poems he had been reading, and piped, 'Why, be

15

welcome, dear boy – Oo-oo-oooh!'

He looked down the muzzle of a blaster.

The man showed teeth. 'Stay right where you are,' he commanded. The vocalizer on his breast rendered the sounds he made into soprano cadenzas and arpeggios, the speech of Lenidel. It could do nothing about his vocabulary and grammar. His knowledge did include the fact that, by omitting all honorifics and circumlocutions without apology, he was uttering a deadly insult.

That was the effect he wanted – deadliness.

'My, my, my dear good friend from the revered Solar Commonwealth,' Witweet stammered, 'is this a, a jest too subtle for a mere pilot like myself to comprehend? I will gladly laugh if you wish, and then we, we shall enjoy tea and cakes. I have genuine Lapsang Soochong tea from Earth, and have just found the most darling recipe for sweet cakes –'

'Quiet!' Harker rapped. His glance flickered to the windows. Outside, flower colors exploded beneath reddish tree trunks; small bright wings went fluttering past; The Waterfall That Rings Like Glass Bells could be heard in the distance. Annanna was akin to most cities of Lenidel, the principal nation on Trillia, in being spread through an immensity of forest and parkscape. Nevertheless, Annanna had a couple of million population, who kept busy. Three aircraft were crossing heaven. At any moment, a pedestrian or cyclist might come along The Pathway Of The Beautiful Blossoms And The Bridge That Arches Like A Note Of Music, and wonder why two humans stood tense outside number 1337.

Witweet regarded the man's skinsuit and boots, the pack on his shoulders, the tightly drawn sharp features behind the weapon. Tears blurred the blue of Witweet's great eyes. 'I fear you are engaged in some desperate undertaking which distorts the natural goodness that, I

16

feel certain, still inheres,' he quavered. 'May I beg the honor of being graciously let help you relieve whatever your distress may be?'

Harker squinted back at the Trillian. *How much do we really know about his breed, anyway? Damned nonhuman thing – Though I never resented his existence till now –* His pulse knocked; his skin was wet and stank, his mouth was dry and cottony-tasting.

Yet his prisoner looked altogether helpless. Witweet was an erect biped; but his tubby frame reached to barely a meter, from the padded feet to the big, scalloped ears. The two arms were broomstick thin, the four fingers on either hand suggested straws. The head was practically spherical, bearing a pug muzzle, moist black nose, tiny mouth, quivering whiskers, upward-slanting tufty brows. That, the tail, and the fluffy silver-gray fur which covered the whole skin, had made Olafsson remark that the only danger to be expected from this race was that eventually their cuteness would become unendurable.

Witweet had nothing upon him except an ornately embroidered kimono and a sash tied in a pink bow. He surely owned no weapons, and probably wouldn't know what to do with any. The Trillians were omnivores, but did not seem to have gone through a hunting stage in their evolution. They had never fought wars, and personal violence was limited to an infrequent scuffle.

Still, Harker thought, *they've shown the guts to push into deep space. I daresay even an unarmed policeman – Courtesy Monitor – could use his vehicle against us, like by ramming.*

Hurry!

'Listen,' he said. 'Listen carefully. You've heard that most intelligent species have members who don't mind using brute force, outright killing, for other ends than self-defense. Haven't you?'

Witweet waved his tail in assent. 'Truly I am baffled by that statement, concerning as it does races whose achievements are of incomparable magnificence. However, not only my poor mind, but those of our most eminent thinkers have been engaged in fruitless endeavors to – '

'Dog your hatch!' The vocalizer made meaningless noises and Harker realized he had shouted in Anglic. He went back to Lenidellian-equivalent. 'I don't propose to waste time. My partners and I did not come here to trade as we announced. We came to get a Trillian spaceship. The project is important enough that we'll kill if we must. Make trouble, and I'll blast you to greasy ash. It won't bother me. And you aren't the only possible pilot we can work through, so don't imagine you can block us by sacrificing yourself. I admit you are our best prospect. Obey, cooperate fully, and you'll live. We'll have no reason to destroy you.' He paused. 'We may even send you home with a good piece of money. We'll be able to afford that.'

The bottling of his fur might have made Witweet impressive to another Trillian. To Harker, he became a ball of fuzz in a kimono, an agitated tail and a sound of coloratura anguish. 'But this is insanity . . . if I may say that to a respected guest . . . One of *our* awkward, lumbering, fragile, unreliable prototype ships – when you came in a vessel representing centuries of advancement – ? Why, why, why, in the name of multiple sacredness, why?'

'I'll tell you later,' the man said. 'You're due for a routine supply trip to, uh, Gwinsai Base, starting tomorrow, right? You'll board this afternoon, to make final inspection and settle in. We're coming along. You'd be leaving in about an hour's time. Your things must already be packed. I didn't cultivate your friendship for nothing, you see! Now, walk slowly ahead of me, bring your luggage back here and open it so I can make sure

18

what you've got. Then we're on our way.'

Witweet stared into the blaster. A shudder went through him. His fur collapsed. Tail dragging, he turned toward the inner rooms.

Stocky Leo Dolgorov and ash-blond Einar Olafsson gusted simultaneous oaths of relief when their leader and his prisoner came out onto the path. 'What took you that time?' the first demanded. 'Were you having a nap?'

'Nah, he entered one of their bowing, scraping, and unction-smearing contests.' Olafsson's grin held scant mirth.

'Trouble?' Harker asked.

'N-no . . . three, four passersby stopped to talk – we told them the story and they went on,' Dolgorov said. Harker nodded. He'd put a good deal of thought into that excuse for his guards' standing around – that they were about to pay a social call on Witweet but were waiting until the pilot's special friend Harker had made him a gift. A lie must be plausible, and the Trillian mind was not human.

'We sure hung on the hook, though.' Olafsson started as a bicyclist came round a bend in the path and fluted a string of complimentary greetings.

Dwarfed beneath the men, Witweet made reply. No gun was pointed at him now, but one rested in each of the holsters near his brain. (Harker and companions had striven to convince everybody that the bearing of arms was a peaceful but highly symbolic custom in *their* part of Technic society, that without their weapons they would feel more indecent than a shaven Trillian.) As far as Harker's wire-taut attention registered, Witweet's answer was routine. But probably some forlornness crept into the overtones, for the neighbor stopped.

'Do you feel quite radiantly well, dear boy?' he asked.

'Indeed I do, honored Pwiddy, and thank you in my

prettiest thoughts for your ever-sweet consideration,' the pilot replied. 'I . . . well, these good visitors from the star-faring culture of splendor have been describing some of their experiences – oh, I simply must relate them to you later, dear boy! – and naturally, since I am about to embark on another trip, I have been made pensive by this.' Hands, tail, whiskers gesticulated. *Meaning what?* wondered Harker in a chill; and clamping jaws together: *Well, you knew you'd have to take risks to win a kingdom.* 'Forgive me, I pray you of your overflowing generosity, that I rush off after such curt words. But I have promises to keep, and considerable distances to go before I sleep.'

'Understood.' Pwiddy spent a mere five minutes bidding farewell all around before he pedaled off. Meanwhile several others passed by. However, since no well-mannered person would interrupt a conversation even to make salute, they created no problem.

'Let's go.' It grated in Dolgorov's throat.

Behind the little witch-hatted house was a pergola wherein rested Witweet's personal flitter. It was large and flashy – large enough for three humans to squeeze into the back – which fact had become an element in Harker's plan. The car that the men had used during their stay on Trillia, they abandoned. It was unmistakably an off-planet vehicle.

'Get started!' Dolgorov cuffed at Witweet.

Olafsson caught his arm and snapped: 'Control your emotions! Want to tear his head off?'

Hunched over the dashboard, Witweet squeezed his eyes shut and shivered till Harker prodded him. 'Pull out of that funk,' the man said.

'I . . . I beg your pardon. The brutality so appalled me – ' Witweet flinched from their laughter. His fingers gripped levers and twisted knobs. Here was no steering by gestures in a light-field, let alone simply speaking an order to an autopilot. The overloaded flitter crawled skyward. Harker detected a flutter in its grav unit, but decided nothing was likely to fail before they reached the spaceport. And after that, nothing would matter except getting off this planet.

Not that it was a bad place, he reflected. Almost Earthlike in size, gravity, air, deliciously edible life forms – an Earth that no longer was and perhaps never had been, wide horizons and big skies, caressed by light and rain. Looking out, he saw woodlands in a thousand hues of green, meadows, river-gleam, an occasional dollhouse dwelling, grainfields ripening tawny and the soft gaudiness of a flower ranch. Ahead lifted The Mountain Which Presides Over Moonrise In Lenidel, a snowpeak pure as Fuji's. The sun, yellower than Sol, turned it and a few clouds into gold.

A gentle world for a gentle people. Too gentle.

Too bad. For them.

Besides, after six months of it, three city-bred men were about ready to climb screaming out of their skulls. Harker drew forth a cigarette, inhaled it into lighting and filled his lungs with harshness. *I'd almost welcome a fight,* he thought savagely.

But none happened. Half a year of hard, patient study paid richly off. It helped that the Trillians were – well, you couldn't say lax about security, because the need for it had never occurred to them. Witweet radioed to the portmaster as he approached, was informed that everything looked okay, and took his flitter straight through an open cargo lock into a hold of the ship he was to pilot.

The port was like nothing in Technic civilization, unless on the remotest, least visited of outposts. After all, the Trillians had gone in a bare fifty years from propeller-driven aircraft to interstellar spaceships. Such concentration on research and development had necessarily been at the expense of production and exploitation. What few vessels they had were still mostly experimental. The scientific bases they had established on planets of next-door stars needed no more than three or four freighters for their maintenance.

Thus a couple of buildings and a ground-control tower bounded a stretch of ferrocrete on a high, chilly plateau; and that was Trillia's spaceport. Two ships were in. One was being serviced, half its hull plates removed and furry shapes swarming over the emptiness within. The other, assigned to Witweet, stood on landing jacks at the far end of the field. Shaped like a fat torpedo, decorated in floral designs of pink and baby blue, it was as big as a Dromond-class hauler. Yet its payload was under a thousand tons. The primitive systems for drive, control, and life support took up that much room.

'I wish you a just too, too delightful voyage,' said the portmaster's voice from the radio. 'Would you honor me by accepting an invitation to dinner? My wife has, if I may boast, discovered remarkable culinary attributes of certain sea weeds brought back from Gwinsai; and for my part, dear boy, I would be so interested to hear your opinion of a new verse form with which I am currently experimenting.'

'No . . . I thank you, no, impossible, I beg indulgence –' It was hard to tell whether the unevenness of Witweet's response came from terror or from the tobacco smoke that had kept him coughing. He almost flung his vehicle into the spaceship.

Clearance granted, *The Serenity of the Estimable Philosopher Ittypu* lifted into a dawn sky. When Trillia was a dwindling cloud-marbled sapphire among the stars, Harker let out a breath. 'We can relax now.'

'Where?' Olafsson grumbled. The single cabin barely allowed three humans to crowd together. They'd have to take turns sleeping in the hall that ran aft to the engine room. And their voyage was going to be long. Top pseudo-velocity under the snail-powered hyperdrive of this craft would be less than one light-year per day.

'Oh, we can admire the darling murals,' Dolgorov fleered. He kicked an intricately painted bulkhead.

Witweet, crouched miserable at the control board, flinched. 'I beg you, dear, kind sir, do not scuff the art-work,' he said.

'Why should you care?' Dolgorov asked. 'You won't be keeping this junkheap.'

Witweet wrung his hands. 'Defacement is still very wicked. Perhaps the consignee will appreciate my pat-terns? I spent *such* a time on them, trying to get every teensiest detail correct.'

'Is that why your freighters have a single person aboard?' Olafsson laughed. 'Always seemed reckless to me, not taking a backup pilot at least. But I suppose two Trillians would get into so fierce an argument about the interior décor that they'd each stalk off in an absolute snit.'

'Why, no,' said Witweet, a trifle calmer. 'We keep personnel down to one because more are not really needed. Piloting between stars is automatic, and the crew-being is trained in servicing functions. Should he suffer harm en route, the ship will put itself into orbit around the destination planet and can be boarded by others. An extra would thus uselessly occupy space which is often needed for passengers. I am surprised that you, sir, who have set a powerful intellect to prolonged consideration of our astronautical practices, should not have been aware – '

'I was, I was!' Olafsson threw up his hands as far as the

overhead permitted. 'Ask a rhetorical question and get an oratorical answer.'

'May I, in turn, humbly request enlightenment as to your reason for . . . sequestering . . . a spacecraft ludicrously inadequate by every standard of your oh, so sophisticated society?'

'You may.' Harker's spirits bubbled from relief of tension. They'd pulled it off. They really had. He sat down – the deck was padded and perfumed – and started a cigarette. Through his bones beat the throb of the gravity drive: energy wasted by a clumsy system. The weight it made underfoot fluctuated slightly in a rhythm that felt wavelike.

'I suppose we may as well call ourselves criminals,' he said; the Lenidellian word he must use had milder connotations. 'There are people back home who wouldn't leave us alive if they knew who'd done certain things. But we never got rich off them. Now we will.'

He had no need for recapitulating except the need to gloat: 'You know we came to Trillia half a standard year ago, on a League ship that was paying a short visit to buy art. We had goods of our own to barter with, and announced we were going to settle down for a while and look into the possibility of establishing a permanent trading post with a regular shuttle service to some of the Technic planets. That's what the captain of the ship thought too. He advised us against it, said it couldn't pay and we'd simply be stuck on Trillia till the next League vessel chanced by, which wouldn't likely be for more than a year. But when we insisted, and gave him passage money, he shrugged,' as did Harker.

'You have told me this,' Witweet said. 'I thrilled to the ecstasy of what I believed was your friendship.'

'Well, I did enjoy your company,' Harker smiled. 'You're not a bad little osco. Mainly, though, we concentrated on you because we'd learned you qualified for our uses – a regular freighter pilot, a bachelor so we needn't fuss with a family, a chatterer who could be pumped for any information we wanted. Seems we gauged well.'

'We better have,' Dolgorov said gloomily. 'Those trade goods cost us everything we could scratch together. I took a steady job for two years, and lived like a lama, to get my share.'

'And now we'll be living like fakirs,' said Olafsson. 'But afterward – afterward!'

'Evidently your whole aim was to acquire a Trillian ship,' Witweet said. 'My bemusement at this endures.'

'We don't actually want the ship as such, except for demonstration purposes,' Harker said. 'What we want is the plans, the design. Between the vessel itself, and the service manuals aboard, we have that in effect.'

Witweet's ears quivered. 'Do you mean to publish the data for scientific interest? Surely, to beings whose ancestors went on to better models centuries ago – if, indeed, they ever burdened themselves with something this crude – surely the interest is nil. Unless . . . you think many will pay to see, in order to enjoy mirth at the spectacle of our fumbling efforts?' He spread his arms. 'Why, you could have bought complete specifications most cheaply; or, indeed, had you requested of me, I would have been bubbly-happy to obtain a set and make you a gift.' On a note of timid hope: 'Thus you see, dear boy, drastic action is quite unnecessary. Let us return. I will state you remained aboard by mistake – '

Olafsson guffawed. Dolgorov said, 'Not even your authorities can be that sloppy-thinking.' Harker ground out his cigarette on the deck, which made the pilot wince, and explained at leisured length:

'We want this ship precisely because it's primitive. Your people weren't in the electronic era when the first human explorers contacted you. They, or some later visitors, brought you texts on physics. Then your bright lads had the theory of such things as gravity control and hyperdrive. But the engineering practice was something else again.

'You didn't have plans for a starship. When you finally got an opportunity to inquire, you found that the idealistic period of Technic civilization was over and you must deal with hardheaded entrepreneurs. And the price was set way beyond what your whole planet could hope to save in League currency. That was just the price for diagrams, not to speak of an actual vessel. I don't know if you are personally aware of the fact – it's no secret – but this is League policy. The member companies are bound by an agreement.

'They won't prevent anyone from entering space on his own. But take your case on Trillia. You had learned in a general way about, oh, transistors, for instance. But that did not set you up to manufacture them. An entire industrial complex is needed for that and for the million other necessary items. To design and build one, with the inevitable mistakes en route, would take decades at a minimum, and would involve regimenting your entire species and living in poverty because every bit of capital has to be reinvested. Well, you Trillians were too sensible to pay that price. You'd proceed more gradually. Yet at the same time, your scientists, all your more adventurous types were burning to get out into space.

'I agree your decision about that was intelligent too. You saw you couldn't go directly from your earliest hydrocarbon-fuelled engines to a modern starship – to a completely integrated system of thermonuclear power-plant, initiative-grade navigation and engineering computers, full-cycle life support, the whole works, using solid-state circuits, molecular-level and nuclear-level transitions, forcefields instead of moving parts – an *organism*, more energy than matter. No, you wouldn't be able to build that for generations, probably.

'But you could go ahead and develop huge, clumsy, but workable fission-power units. You could use vacuum tubes, glass rectifiers, kilometers of wire, to generate and regulate the necessary forces. You could store data on tape if not in single molecules, retrieve with a cathode-ray scanner if not with a quantum-field pulse, compute with miniaturized gas-filled units that react in microseconds if not with photon interplays that take a nanosecond.

'You're like islanders who had nothing better than canoes till someone happened by in a nuclear-powered submarine. They couldn't copy that, but they might invent a reciprocating steam engine turning a screw – they might attach an airpipe so it could submerge – and it wouldn't impress the outsiders, but it would cross the ocean too, at its own pace; and it would overawe any neighboring tribes.'

He stopped for breath.

'I see,' Witweet murmured slowly. His tail switched back and forth. 'You can sell our designs to sophonts in a proto-industrial stage of technological development. The idea comes from an excellent brain. But why could you not simply buy the plans for resale elsewhere?'

'The damned busybody League.' Dolgorov spat.

'The fact is,' Olafsson said, 'spacecraft – of advanced type – have been sold to, ah, less advanced peoples in the past. Some of those weren't near industrialization, they were Iron Age barbarians, whose only thought was plundering and conquering. They could do that, given ships which are practically self-piloting, self-maintaining, self-everything. It's cost a good many lives and heavy material losses on border planets. But at least none of the barbarians have been able to duplicate the craft thus far.

27

Hunt every pirate and warlord down, and that ends the problem. Or so the League hopes. It's banned any more such trades.'

He cleared his throat. 'I don't refer to races like the Trillians, who're obviously capable of reaching the stars by themselves and unlikely to be a menace when they do,' he said. 'You're free to buy anything you can pay for. The price of certain things is set astronomical mainly to keep you from beginning overnight to compete with the old-established outfits. They prefer a gradual phasing-in of newcomers, so they can adjust.

'But aggressive, warlike cultures, that'd not be interested in reaching a peaceful accommodation – they're something else again. There's a total prohibition on supplying their sort with anything that might lead to them getting off their planets in less than centuries. If League agents catch you at it, they don't fool around with rehabilitation like a regular government. They shoot you.'

Harker grimaced. 'I saw once on a telescreen interview,' he remarked, 'Old Nick van Rijn said he wouldn't shoot that kind of offenders. He'd hang them. A rope is reusable.'

'And this ship *can* be copied,' Witweet breathed. 'A low industrial technology, lower than ours, could tool up to produce a modified design, in a comparatively short time, if guided by a few engineers from the core civilization.'

'I trained as an engineer,' Harker said. 'Likewise Leo; and Einar spent several years on a planet where one royal family has grandiose ambitions.'

'But the horror you would unleash!' wailed the Trillian. He stared into their stoniness. 'You would never dare go home,' he said.

'Don't want to anyway,' Harker answered. 'Power, wealth, yes, and everything those will buy – we'll have more than we can use up in our lifetimes, at the court of the Militants. Fun, too.' He smiled. 'A challenge, you know, to build a space navy from zero. I expect to enjoy my work.'

'Will not the, the, the Polesotechnic League . . . take measures?'

'That's why we must operate as we have done. They'd learn about a sale of plans, and then they wouldn't stop till they'd found and suppressed our project. But a non-Technic ship that never reported in won't interest them. Our destination is well outside their sphere of normal operations. They needn't discover any hint of what's going on – till an interstellar empire too big for them to break is there. Meanwhile, as we gain resources, we'll have been modernizing our industry and fleet.'

'It's all arranged,' Olafsson said. 'The day we show up in the land of the Militants, bringing the ship we described to them, we'll become princes.'

'Kings, later,' Dolgorov added. 'Behave accordingly, you xeno. We don't need you much. I'd soon as not boot you through an airlock.'

Witweet spent minutes just shuddering.

The Serenity, etc., moved on away from Trillia's golden sun. It had to reach a weaker gravitational field than a human craft would have needed, before its hyperdrive would function.

Harker spent part of that period being shown around, top to bottom and end to end. He'd toured a sister ship before, but hadn't dared ask for demonstrations as thorough as he now demanded. 'I want to know this monstrosity we've got, inside out,' he said while personally tearing down and rebuilding a cumbersome oxygen renewer. He could do this because most equipment was paired, against the expectation of eventual in-flight down time.

In a hold, among cases of supplies for the research team on Gwinsai, he was surprised to recognize a lean cylindroid, one hundred twenty centimeters long. 'But here's a Solar-built courier!' he exclaimed.

Witweet made eager gestures of agreement. He'd been falling over himself to oblige his captors. 'For messages in case of emergency, magnificent sir,' he babbled. 'A hyperdrive unit, an autopilot, a radio to call at journey's end till someone comes and retrieves the enclosed letter – '

'I know, I know. But why not build your own?'

'Well, if you will deign to reflect upon the matter, you will realize that anything we could build would be too slow and unreliable to afford very probable help. Especially since it is most unlikely that, at any given time, another spaceship would be ready to depart Trillia on the instant. Therefore this courier is set, as you can see if you wish to examine the program, to go a considerably greater distance – though nevertheless not taking long, your human constructions being superlatively fast – to the planet called, ah, Oasis . . . and Anglic word meaning a lovely, cool, refreshing haven, am I correct?'

Harker nodded impatiently. 'Yes, one of the League companies does keep a small base there.'

'We have arranged that they will send aid if requested. At a price, to be sure. However, for our poor economy, as ridiculous a hulk as this is still a heavy investment, worth insuring.'

'I see. I didn't know you bought such gadgets – not that there'd be a pegged price on them; they don't matter any more than spices or medical equipment. Of course, I couldn't find out every detail in advance, especially not things you people take so for granted that you didn't think to mention them.' On impulse, Harker patted the round head. 'You know, Witweet, I guess I do like you. I will see you're rewarded for your help.'

'Passage home will suffice,' the Trillian said quietly, 'though I do not know how I can face my kinfolk after having been the instrument of death and ruin for millions of innocents.'

'Then don't go home,' Harker suggested. 'We can't release you for years in any case, to blab our scheme and our coordinates. But we could smuggle in whatever and whoever you wanted, same as for ourselves.'

The head rose beneath his palm as the slight form straightened. 'Very well,' Witweet declared.

That fast? jarred through Harker. *He is nonhuman, yes, but –* The wondering was dissipated by the continuing voice:

'Actually, dear boy, I must disabuse you. We did not buy our couriers, we salvaged them.'

'What? Where?'

'Have you heard of a planet named, by its human discoverers, Paradox?'

Harker searched his memory. Before leaving Earth he had consulted every record he could find about this entire stellar neighborhood. Poorly known though it was to men, there had been a huge mass of data – suns, worlds . . . 'I think so,' he said. 'Big, isn't it? With, uh, a freaky atmosphere.'

'Yes.' Witweet spoke rapidly. 'It gave the original impetus to Technic exploration of our vicinity. But later the men departed. In recent years, when we ourselves became able to pay visits, we found their abandoned camp. A great deal of gear had been left behind, presumably because it was designed for Paradox only and would be of no use elsewhere, hence not worth hauling back. Among these machines we came upon a few couriers. I suppose they had been overlooked. Your civilization can afford

31

profligacy, if I may use that term in due respectfulness.'

He crouched, as if expecting a blow. His eyes glittered in the gloom of the hold.

'Hm.' Harker frowned. 'I suppose by now you've stripped the place.'

'Well, no.' Witweet brushed nervously at his rising fur. 'Like the men, we saw no use in, for example, tractors designed for a gravity of two-point-eight terrestrial. They can operate well and cheaply on Paradox, since their fuel is crude oil, of which an abundant supply exists near the campsite. But we already had electric-celled grav motors, however archaic they are by your standards. And we do not need weapons like those we found, presumably for protection against animals. We certainly have no intention of colonizing Paradox!'

'Hm.' The human waved, as if to brush off the chattering voice. 'Hm.' He slouched off, hands in pockets, pondering.

In the time that followed, he consulted the navigator's bible. His reading knowledge of Lenidellian was fair. The entry for Paradox was as laconic as it would have been in a Technic reference; despite the limited range of their operations, the Trillians had already encountered too many worlds to allow flowery descriptions. Star type and coordinates, orbital elements, mass density, atmospheric composition, temperature ranges, and the usual rest were listed. There was no notation about habitability, but none was needed. The original explorers hadn't been poisoned or come down with disease; Trillian metabolism was similar to theirs.

The gravity field was not too strong for this ship to make landing and, later, ascent. Weather shouldn't pose any hazards, given reasonable care in choosing one's path; that was a weakly energized environment. Besides, the vessel was meant for planetfalls, and Witweet was a skilled pilot in his fashion . . .

Harker discussed the idea with Olafsson and Dolgorov. 'It won't take but a few days,' he said, 'and we might pick up something really good. You know I've not been too happy about the Militants' prospects of building an ample industrial base fast enough to suit us. Well, a few machines like this, simply things they can easily copy but designed by good engineers . . . could make a big difference.'

'They're probably rustheaps,' Dolgorov snorted. 'That was long ago.'

'No, durable alloys were available then,' Olafsson said. 'I like the notion intrinsically, Bryce. I don't like the thought of our tame xeno taking us down. He might crash us on purpose.'

'That sniveling faggot?' Dolgorov gibed. He jerked his head backward at Witweet, who sat enormous-eyed in the pilot chair listening to a language he did not understand. 'By accident, maybe, seeing how scared he is!'

'It's a risk we take at journey's end,' Harker reminded them. 'Not a real risk. The ship has some ingenious failsafes built in. Anyhow, I intend to stand over him the whole way down. If he does a single thing wrong, I'll kill him. The controls aren't made for me, but I can get us aloft again, and afterward we can re-rig.'

Olafsson nodded. 'Seems worth a try,' he said. 'What can we lose except a little time and sweat?'

Paradox rolled enormous in the viewscreen, a darkling world, the sky-band along its sunrise horizon redder than Earth's, polar caps and winter snowfields gashed by the teeth of mountains, tropical forest and pampas a yellow-brown fading into raw deserts on one side and chopped off on another side by the furious surf of an ocean where three moons fought their tidal wars. The sun was distance-dwarfed, more dull in hue than Sol, nevertheless too bright to look near. Elsewhere, stars filled illimitable blackness.

It was very quiet aboard, save for the mutter of power-plant and ventilators, the breathing of men, their restless shuffling about in the cramped cabin. The air was blued and fouled by cigarette smoke; Witweet would have fled into the corridor, but they made him stay, clutching a perfume-dripping kerchief to his nose.

Harker straightened from the observation screen. Even at full magnification, the rudimentary electro-optical system gave little except blurriness. But he'd practiced on it, while orbiting a satellite, till he felt he could read those wavering traces.

'Campsite and machinery, all right,' he said. 'No details. Brush has covered everything. When were your people here last, Witweet?'

'Several years back,' the Trillian wheezed. 'Evidently vegetation grows apace. Do you agree on the safety of a landing?'

'Yes. We may snap a few branches, as well as flatten a lot of shrubs, but we'll back down slowly, the last hundred meters, and we'll keep the radar, sonar, and gravar sweeps going.' Harker glanced at his men. 'Next thing is to compute our descent pattern,' he said. 'But first I want to spell out again, point by point, exactly what each of us is to do under exactly what circumstances. I don't aim to take chances.'

'Oh, no,' Witweet squeaked. 'I beg you, dear boy, I beg you the prettiest I can, please don't.'

After the tension of transit, landing was an anticlimax. All at once the engine fell silent. A wind whistled around the hull. Viewscreens showed low, thick-boled trees; fronded

34

brownish leaves; tawny undergrowth; shadowy glimpses of metal objects beneath vines and amidst tall, whipping stalks. The sun stood at late afternoon in a sky almost purple.

Witweet checked the indicators while Harker studied them over his head. 'Air breathable, of course,' the pilot said, 'which frees us of the handicap of having to wear smelly old spacesuits. We should bleed it in gradually, since the pressure is greater than ours at present and we don't want earaches, do we? Temperature – ' He shivered delicately. 'Be certain you are wrapped up snug before you venture outside.'

'You're venturing first,' Harker informed him.

'What? Oo-ooh, my good, sweet, darling friend, no, please, no! It is *cold* out there, scarcely above freezing. And once on the ground, no gravity generator to help, why, weight will be tripled. What could I possibly, possibly do? No, let me stay inside, keep the home fires burning – I mean keep the thermostat at a cozy temperature – and, yes, I will make you the nicest pot of tea – '

'If you don't stop fluttering and do what you're told, I'll tear your head off,' Dolgorov said. 'Guess what I'll use your skin for.'

'Let's get cracking,' Olafsson said. 'I don't want to stay in this Helheim any longer than you.'

They opened a hatch the least bit. While Paradoxian air seeped in, they dressed as warmly as might be, except for Harker. He intended to stand by the controls for the first investigatory period. The entering gases added a whine to the wind-noise. Their helium content made speech and other sounds higher pitched, not quite natural; and this would have to be endured for the rest of the journey, since the ship had insufficient reserve tanks to flush out the new atmosphere. A breath of cold got by the heaters, and a rank smell of alien growth.

But you could get used to hearing funny, Harker thought. And the native life might stink, but it was harmless. You couldn't eat it and be nourished, but neither could its germs live off your body. If heavy weapons had been needed here, they were far more likely against large, blundering herbivores than against local tigers.

That didn't mean they couldn't be used in war.

Trembling, eyes squinched half-shut, tail wrapped around his muzzle, the rest of him bundled in four layers of kimono, Witweet crept to the personnel lock. Its outer valve swung wide. The gangway went down. Harker grinned to see the dwarfish shape descend, step by step under the sudden harsh hauling of the planet.

'Sure you can move around in that pull?' he asked his companions.

'Sure,' Dolgorov grunted. 'An extra hundred-fifty kilos? I can backpack more than that, and then it's less well distributed.'

'Stay cautious, though. Too damned easy to fall and break bones.'

'I'd worry more about the cardiovascular system,' Olafsson said. 'One can stand three gees a while, but not for a very long while. Fluid begins seeping out of the cell walls, the heart feels the strain too much – and we've no gravanol along as the first expedition must have had.'

'We'll only be here a few days at most,' Harker said, 'with plenty of chances to rest inboard.'

'Right,' Olafsson agreed. 'Forward!'

Gripping his blaster, he shuffled forward on to the gangway. Dolgorov followed. Below, Witweet huddled. Harker looked out at bleakness, felt the wind slap his face with chill, and was glad he could stay behind. Later he must take his turn outdoors, but for now he could enjoy warmth, decent weight –

The world reached up and grabbed him. Off balance, he

fell to the deck. His left hand struck first, pain gushed, he saw the wrist and arm splinter. He screamed. The sound came weak as well as shrill, out of a breast laboring against thrice the heaviness it should have had. At the same time, the lights in the ship went out.

Witweet perched on a boulder. His back was straight in spite of the drag on him, which made his robes hang stiff as if carved on an idol of some minor god of justice. His tail, erect, blew jauntily in the bitter sunset wind; the colors of his garments were bold against murk that rose in the forest around the dead spacecraft.

He looked into the guns of three men, and into the terror that had taken them behind the eyes; and Witweet laughed.

'Put those toys away before you hurt yourselves,' he said, using no circumlocutions or honorifics.

'You bastard, you swine, you filthy treacherous xeno, I'll kill you,' Dolgorov groaned. 'Slowly.'

'First you must catch me,' Witweet answered. 'By virtue of being small, I have a larger surface-to-volume ratio than you. My bones, my muscles, my veins and capillaries and cell membranes suffer less force per square centimeter than do yours. I can move faster than you, here. I can survive longer.'

'You can't outrun a blaster bolt,' Olafsson said.

'No. You can kill me with that – a quick, clean death which does not frighten me. Really, because we of Lenidel observe certain customs of courtesy, use certain turns of speech – because our males in particular are encouraged to develop esthetic interests and compassion – does that mean we are cowardly or effeminate?' The Trillian clicked his tongue. 'If you supposed so, you committed an elementary logical fallacy which our philosophers name the does-not-follow.'

37

'Why shouldn't we kill you?'

'That is inadvisable. You see, your only hope is quick rescue by a League ship. The courier can operate here, being a solid-state device. It can reach Oasis and summon a vessel which, itself of similar construction, can also land on Paradox and take off again . . . in time. This would be impossible for a Trillian craft. Even if one were ready to leave, I doubt the Astronautical Senate would permit the pilot to risk descent.

'Well, rescuers will naturally ask questions. I cannot imagine any story which you three men, alone, might concoct that would stand up under the subsequent, inevitable investigation. On the other hand, I can explain to the League's agents that you were only coming along to look into trade possibilities and that we were trapped on Paradox by a faulty autopilot which threw us into a descent curve. I can do this *in detail*, which you could not if you killed me. They will return us all to Trillia, where there is no death penalty.'

Witweet smoothed his wind-ruffled whiskers. 'The alternative,' he finished, 'is to die where you are, in a most unpleasant fashion.'

Harker's splinted arm gestured back the incoherent Dolgorov. He set an example by holstering his own gun. 'I . . . guess we're outsmarted,' he said, word by foultasting word. 'But what happened? Why's the ship inoperable?'

'Helium in the atmosphere,' Witweet explained calmly. 'The monatomic helium molecule is ooh-how-small. It diffuses through almost every material. Vacuum tubes, glass rectifiers, electronic switches dependent on pure gases, any such device soon becomes poisoned. You, who were used to a technology that had long left this kind of thing behind, did not know the fact, and it did not occur to you as a possibility. We Trillians are, of course, rather acutely aware of the problem. I am the first who ever set foot on Paradox. You should have noted that my courier is a present-day model.'

'I see,' Olafsson mumbled.

'The sooner we get our message off, the better,' Witweet said. 'By the way, I assume you are not so foolish as to contemplate the piratical takeover of a vessel of the Polesotechnic League.'

'Oh, no!' said they, including Dolgorov, and the other two blasters were sheathed.

'One thing, though,' Harker said. A part of him wondered if the pain in him was responsible for his own abnormal self-possession. Counterirritant against dismay? Would he weep after it wore off? 'You bargain for your life by promising to have ours spared. How do we know we want your terms? What'll they do to us on Trillia?'

'Entertain no fears,' Witweet assured him. 'We are not vindictive, as I have heard some species are; nor have we any officious concept of "rehabilitation". Wrongdoers are required to make amends to the fullest extent possible. You three have cost my people a valuable ship and whatever cargo cannot be salvaged. You must have technological knowledge to convey, of equal worth. The working conditions will not be intolerable. Probably you can make restitution and win release before you reach old age.

'Now, come, get busy. First we dispatch that courier, then we prepare what is necessary for our survival until rescue.'

He hopped down from the rock, which none of them would have been able to do unscathed, and approached them through gathering cold twilight with the stride of a conqueror.

A book such as this would be rattlewing indeed did it not tell anything about Falkayn himself. Yet there seems no lift in repeating common knowledge or reprinting tales which, in their different versions, are as popular and available as ever aforetime.

Therefore Hloch reckons himself fortunate in having two stories whereof the fullness is well-nigh unknown, and which furthermore deal with events whose consequences are still breeding winds.

The first concerns Merseia. Although most folk, even here on far Avalon, have caught some awareness of yonder world and the strange fate that stooped upon it, the part that the Founder-to-be took has long been shadowed, as has been the very fact that he was there at all. For reasons of discretion, he never spoke publicly of the matter, and his report was well buried in League archives. Among his descendants, only a vague tradition remained that he had passed through such air.

Hearing this, Rennhi set herself to hunt down the truth. On Falkayn's natal planet Hermes she learned that, several years after the Babur War, he and van Rijn had quietly transferred many data units thither, putting them in care of the Grand Ducal house and his own immediate kin. The feeling was that they would be more secure than in the Solar System, now when a time of storms was so clearly brewing. After the League broke up, there was no decipherment program anymore, and the units lay virtually forgotten in storage. Rennhi won permission to transfer the molecular patterns. Once home again, she instigated a code-breaking effort. It was supported by the armed forces in hopes of snatching useful information, for by that time war with the Empire had become a thunderhead threat.

This hope was indirectly fulfilled. Nothing in the records had military value but the cracking of a fiendishly clever cipher developed cryptographic capabilities. Nor does much in them have any particular bearing on Avalon. Nearly everything deals with details of matters whose bones grew white centuries ago. Interrupted by hostilities, the study has only been completed lately.

A few treasures did come forth, bright among them a full account of what happened on Merseia. Hloch and Arinnian together have worked it into narrative form.

DAY OF BURNING

For who knows how long, the star had orbited quietly in the wilderness between Betelgeuse and Rigel. It was rather more massive than average – about half again as much as Sol – and shone with corresponding intensity, white-hot, corona and prominences a terrible glory. But there are no few like it. A ship of the first Grand Survey noted its existence. However, the crew were more interested in a neighbor sun which had planets, and could not linger long in that system either. The galaxy is too big; their purpose was to get some hint about this spiral arm which we inhabit. Thus certain spectroscopic omens escaped their notice.

No one returned thither for a pair of centuries. Technic civilization had more than it could handle, let alone comprehend, in the millions of stars closer to home. So the fact remained unsuspected that this one was older than normal for its type in its region, must indeed have wandered in from other parts. Not that it was very ancient, astronomically speaking. But the great childless suns evolve fast and strangely.

By chance, though, a scout from the Polesotechnic League, exploring far in search of new markets, was passing within a light-year when the star exploded.

Say instead (insofar as simultaneity has any meaning across interstellar distances) that the death agony had occurred some months before. Even more fierce, thermonuclear reaction had burned up the last hydrogen at the center. Unbalanced by radiation pressure, the outer layers collapsed beneath their own weight. Forces were released which triggered a wholly different order of atomic fusions. New elements came into being, not only those which may be found in the planets but also the short-lived transuranics; for a while, technetium itself dominated that anarchy. Neutrons and neutrinos flooded forth, carrying with them the last balancing energy. Compression turned into catastrophe. At the brief peak, the supernova was as radiant as its entire galaxy.

So close, the ship's personnel would have died had she not been in hyperdrive. They did not remain there. A dangerous amount of radiation was still touching them between quantum microjumps. And they were not equipped to study the phenomenon. This was the first chance in our history to observe a new supernova. Earth was too remote to help. But the scientific colony on Catawrayannis could be reached fairly soon. It could dispatch laboratory craft.

Now to track in detail what was going to happen, considerable resources were demanded. Among these were a place where men could live and instruments be made to order as the need for them arose. Such things could not well be sent from the usual factories. By the time they arrived, the wave front carrying information about rapidly progressing events would have traveled so far that inversesquare enfeeblement would create maddening inaccuracies.

But a little beyond one parsec from the star – an excellent distance for observation over a period of years – was a G-type sun. One of its planets was terrestroid to numerous points of classification, both physically and biochemically. Survey records showed that the most advanced culture on it was at the verge of an industrial-scientific revolution. Ideal!

Except, to be sure, that Survey's information was less than sketchy, and two centuries out of date.

'No.'

Master Merchant David Falkayn stepped backward in startlement. The four nearest guards clutched at their pistols. Peripherally and profanely, Falkayn wondered what canon he had violated now.

'Beg, uh, beg pardon?' he fumbled.

Morruchan Long-Ax, the Hand of the Vach Dathyr, leaned forward on his dais. He was big even for a Merseian, which meant that he overtopped Falkayn's rangy height by a good fifteen centimeters. Long, shoulder-flared orange robes and horned miter made his bulk almost overwhelming. Beneath them, he was approximately anthropoid, save for a slanting posture counterbalanced by the tail which, with his booted feet, made a tripod for him to sit on. The skin was green, faintly scaled, totally hairless. A spiky ridge ran from the top of his skull to the end of that tail. Instead of earflaps, he had deep convolutions in his head. But the face was manlike, in a heavy-boned fashion, and the physiology was essentially mammalian.

How familiar the mind was, behind those jet eyes, Falkayn did not know.

The harsh basso said: 'You shall not take the rule of this world. If we surrendered the right and freehold they won, the God would cast back the souls of our

45

ancestors to shriek at us.'

Falkayn's glance flickered around. He had seldom felt so alone. The audience chamber of Castle Afon stretched high and gaunt, proportioned like nothing men had ever built. Curiously woven tapestries on the stone walls, between windows arched at both top and bottom, and battle banners hung from the rafters, did little to stop echoes. The troopers lining the hall, down to a hearth whose fire could have roasted an elephant, wore armor and helmets with demon masks. The guns which they added to curved swords and barbed pikes did not seem out of place. Rather, what appeared unattainably far was a glimpse of ice-blue sky outside.

The air was chill with winter. Gravity was little higher than Terrestrial, but Falkayn felt it dragging at him.

He straightened. He had his own sidearm, no chemical slugthrower but an energy weapon. Adzel, abroad in the city, and Chee Lan aboard the ship, were listening in via the transceiver on his wrist. And the ship had power to level all Ardaig. Morruchan must realize as much.

But he had to be made to cooperate.

Falkayn picked his words with care: 'I pray forgiveness, Hand, if perchance in mine ignorance I misuse thy . . . uh . . . your tongue. Naught was intended save friendliness. Hither bring I news of peril impending, for the which ye must busk yourselves betimes lest ye lose everything ye possess. My folk would fain show your folk what to do. So vast is the striving needed, and so scant the time, that perforce ye must take our counsel. Else can we be of no avail. But never will we act as conquerors. 'Twere not simply an evil deed, but 'twould boot us naught, whose trafficking is with many worlds. Nay, we would be brothers, come to help in a day of sore need.'

Morruchan scowled and rubbed his chin. 'Say on, then,' he replied. 'Frankly, I am dubious. You claim Valenderay is about to become a supernova –'

'Nay, Hand, I declare it hath already done so. The light therefrom will smite this planet in less than three years.'

The time unit Falkayn actually used was Merseian, a trifle greater than Earth's. He sweated and swore to himself at the language problem. The Survey xenologists had gotten a fair grasp of Eriau in the several months they spent here, and Falkayn and his shipmates had acquired it by synapse transform while en route. But now it turned out that, two hundred years back, Eriau had been in a state of linguistic overturn. He wasn't even pronouncing the vowels right.

He tried to update his grammar. 'Would ye, uh, I mean if your desire is . . . if you want confirmation, we can take you or a trusty member of your household so near in our vessel that the starburst is beheld with living eyes.'

'No doubt the scientists and poets will duel for a berth on that trip,' Morruchan said in a dry voice. 'But I believe you already. You yourself, your ship and companions, are proof.' His tone sharpened. 'At the same time, I am no Believer, imagining you half-divine because you come from outside. Your civilization has a technological head start on mine, nothing else. A careful reading of the records from that other brief period when aliens dwelt among us shows they had no reason more noble than professional curiosity. And that was fitful; they left, and none ever returned. Until now.

'So: what do you want from us?'

Falkayn relaxed a bit. Morruchan seemed to be his own kind despite everything, not awestruck, not idealistic, not driven by some incomprehensible nonhuman motivation, but a shrewd and skeptical politician of a pragmatically oriented culture.

Seems to be, the man cautioned himself. *What do I really know about Merseia?*

Judging by observation made in orbit, radio monitoring, initial radio contact, and the ride here in an electric groundcar, this planet still held a jumble of societies, dominated by the one which surrounded the Wilwidh Ocean. Two centuries ago, local rule had been divided among aristocratic clans. He supposed that a degree of continental unification had since been achieved, for his request for an interview with the highest authority had gotten him to Ardaig and a confrontation with this individual. But could Morruchan speak for his entire species? Falkayn doubted it.

Nevertheless, you had to start somewhere.

'I shall be honest, Hand,' he said. 'My crew and I are come as naught but preparers of the way. Can we succeed, we will be rewarded with a share in whatever gain ensueth. For our scientists wish to use Merseia and its moons as bases wherefrom to observe the supernova through the next dozen years. Best for them would be if you folk could provide them with most of their needs, not alone food but such instruments as they tell you how to fashion. For this they will pay fairly; and in addition, ye will acquire knowledge.

'Yet first must we assure that there remaineth a Merseian civilization. To do that, we must wreak huge works. And ye will pay us for our toil and goods supplied to that end. The price will not be usurious, but it will allow us a profit. Out of it, we will buy whatever Merseian wares can be sold at home for further profit.' He smiled. 'Thus all may win and none need fear. The Polesotechnic League compriseth not conquerors nor bandits, naught save merchant adventurers who seek to make their' – more or less – 'honest living.'

'*Hunh!*' Morruchan growled. 'Now we bite down to the bone. When you first communicated and spoke about a supernova, my colleagues and I consulted the astronom-

48

ers. We are not altogether savages here; we have at least gone as far as atomic power and interplanetary travel. Well, our astronomers said that such a star reaches a peak output about fifteen billion times as great as Korych. Is this right?'

'Close enough, Hand, if Korych be your own sun.'

'The only nearby one which might burst in this manner is Valenderay. From your description, the brightest in the southern sky, you must be thinking of it too.'

Falkayn nodded, realized he wasn't sure if this gesture meant the same thing on Merseia, remembered it did, and said: 'Aye, Hand.'

'It sounded terrifying,' Morruchan said, 'until they pointed out that Valenderay is three and a half light-years distant. And this is a reach so enormous that no mind can swallow it. The radiation, when it gets to us, will equal a mere one-third of what comes daily from Korych. And in some fifty-five days' (Terrestrial) 'it will have dwindled to half . . . and so on, until before long we see little except a bright nebula at night.

'True, we can expect troublesome weather, storms, torrential rains, perhaps some flooding if sufficient of the south polar ice cap melts. But that will pass. In any case, the center of civilization is here, in the northern hemisphere. It is also true that, at peak, there will be a dangerous amount of ultraviolet and X radiation. But Merseia's atmosphere will block it.

'Thus.' Morruchan leaned back on his tail and bridged the fingers of his oddly humanlike hands. 'The peril you speak of scarcely exists. What do you really want?'

Falkayn's boyhood training, as a nobleman's son on Hermes, rallied within him. He squared his shoulders. He was not unimpressive, a tall, fair-haired young man with blue eyes bright in a lean, high-cheekboned face. 'Hand,' he said gravely, 'I perceive you have not yet had time to consult your folk who are wise in matters – '

And then he broke down. He didn't know the word for 'electronic'.

Morruchan refrained from taking advantage. Instead, the Merseian became quite helpful. Falkayn's rejoinder was halting, often interrupted while he and the other worked out what a phrase must be. But, in essence and in current language, what he said was:

'The Hand is correct as far as he goes. But consider what will follow. The eruption of a supernova is violent beyond imagining. Nuclear processes are involved, so complex that we ourselves don't yet understand them in detail. That's why we want to study them. But this much we do know, and your physicists will confirm it.

'As nuclei and electrons recombine in that supernal fireball, they generate asymmetrical magnetic pulses. Surely you know what this does when it happens in the detonation of an atomic weapon. Now think of it on a stellar scale. When those forces hit, they will blast straight through Merseia's own magnetic field, down to the very surface. Unshielded electric motors, generators, transmission lines . . . oh, yes, no doubt you have surge arrestors, but your circuit breakers will be tripped, intolerable voltages will be induced, the entire system will be wrecked. Likewise telecommunications lines. And computers. If you use transistors – ah, you do – the flipflop between p and n type conduction will wipe every memory bank, stop every operation in its tracks.

'Electrons, riding that magnetic pulse, will not be long in arriving. As they spiral in the planet's field, their synchrotron radiation will completely blanket whatever electronic apparatus you may have salvaged. Protons should be slower, pushed to about half the speed of light. Then come the alpha particles, then the heavier matter:

50

year after year after year of cosmic fallout, most of it radioactive, to a total greater by orders of magnitude than any war could create before civilization was destroyed. Your planetary magnetism is no real shield. The majority of ions are energetic enough to get through. Nor is your atmosphere any good defense. Heavy nuclei, sleeting through it, will produce secondary radiation that does reach the ground.

'I do not say this planet will be wiped clean of life. But I do say that, without ample advance preparation, it will suffer ecological disaster. Your species might or might not survive; but if you do, it will be as a few starveling primitives. The early breakdown of the electric systems on which your civilization is now dependent will have seen to that. Just imagine. Suddenly no more food moves into the cities. The dwellers go forth as a ravening horde. But if most of your farmers are as specialized as I suppose, they won't even be able to support themselves. Once fighting and famine have become general, no more medical service will be possible, and the pestilences will start. It will be like the aftermath of an all-out nuclear strike against a country with no civil defense. I gather you've avoided that on Merseia. But you certainly have theoretical studies of the subject, and – I have seen planets where it did happen.

'Long before the end, your colonies throughout this system will have been destroyed by the destruction of the apparatus that keeps the colonists alive. And for many years, no spaceship will be able to move.

'Unless you accept our help. We know how to generate force screens, small ones for machines, gigantic ones which can give an entire planet some protection. Not enough – but we also know how to insulate against the energies that get through. We know how to build engines and communications lines which are not affected. We know how to sow substances which protect life against hard radiation. We know how to restore mutated genes. In short, we have the knowledge you need for survival.

'The effect will be enormous. Most of it you must carry out yourselves. Our available personnel are too few, our lines of interstellar transportation too long. But we can supply engineers and organizers.

'To be blunt, Hand, you are very lucky that we learned of this in time, barely in time. Don't fear us. We have no ambitions toward Merseia. If nothing else, it lies far beyond our normal sphere of operation, and we have millions of more profitable planets much closer to home. We want to save you, because you are sentient beings. But it'll be expensive, and a lot of the work will have to be done by outfits like mine, which exist to make a profit. So, besides a scientific base, we want a reasonable economic return.

'Eventually, though, we'll depart. What you do then is your own affair. But you'll still have your civilization. You'll also have a great deal of new equipment and new knowledge. I think you're getting a bargain.'

Falkayn stopped. For a while, silence dwelt in that long dim hall. He grew aware of odors which had never been on Earth or Hermes.

Morruchan said at last, slowly: 'This must be thought on. I shall have to confer with my colleagues, and others. There are so many complications. For example, I see no good reason to do anything for the colony on Ronruad, and many excellent reasons for letting it die.'

'What?' Falkayn's teeth clicked together. 'Meaneth the Hand the next outward planet? But meseems faring goeth on apace throughout this system.'

'Indeed, indeed,' Morruchan said impatiently. 'We depend on the other planets for a number of raw materials, like fissionables, or complex gases from the outer

worlds. Ronruad, though, is of use only to the Gethfennu.'

He spoke that word with such distaste that Falkayn
postponed asking for a definition. 'What recommendations I make in my report will draw heavily upon the
Hand's wisdom,' the human said.

'Your courtesy is appreciated,' Morruchan replied:
with how much irony, Falkayn wasn't sure. He was taking
the news more coolly than expected. But then, he was of
a different race from men, and a soldierly tradition as
well. 'I hope that, for now, you will honor the Vach
Dathyr by guesting us.'

'Well – ' Falkayn hesitated. He had planned on returning to his ship. But he might do better on the spot. The
Survey crew had found Merseian food nourishing to men,
in fact tasty. One report had waxed ecstatic about the ale.

'I thank the Hand.'

'Good. I suggest you go to the chambers already prepared, to rest and refresh yourself. With your leave, a
messenger will come presently to ask what he should
bring you from your vessel. Unless you wish to move it
here?'

'Uh, best not ... policy – ' Falkayn didn't care to take
chances. The Merseians were not so far behind the
League that they couldn't spring a nasty surprise if they
wanted to.

Morruchan raised the skin above his brow ridges but
made no comment. 'You will dine with me and my coun-
cillors at sunset,' he said. They parted ceremoniously.

A pair of guards conducted Falkayn out, through a
series of corridors and up a sweeping staircase whose
bannister was carved into the form of a snake. At the end,
he was ushered into a suite. The rooms were spacious,
their comfort-making gadgetry not greatly below Technic
standards. Reptile-skin carpets and animal skulls

53

mounted on the crimson-draped walls were a little disquieting, but what the hell. A balcony gave on a view of the palace gardens, whose austere good taste was reminiscent of Original Japanese, and on the city.

Ardaig was sizeable, must hold two or three million souls. This quarter was ancient, with buildings of gray stone fantastically turreted and battlemented. The hills which ringed it were checkered by the estates of the wealthy. Snow lay white and blue-shadowed between. Ramparted with tall modern structures, the bay shone like gunmetal. Cargo ships moved in and out, a delta-wing jet whistled overhead. But he heard little traffic noise; nonessential vehicles were banned in the sacred Old Quarter.

'Wedhi is my name, Protector,' said the short Merseian in the black tunic who had been awaiting him. 'May he consider me his liegeman, to do as he commands.' Tail slapped ankles in salute.

'My thanks,' Falkayn said. 'Thou mayest show me how one maketh use of facilities.' He couldn't wait to see a bathroom designed for these people. 'And then, mayhap, a tankard of beer, a textbook on political geography, and privacy for some hours.'

'The Protector has spoken. If he will follow me?'

The two of them entered the adjoining chamber, which was furnished for sleeping. As if by accident, Wedhi's tail brushed the door. It wasn't automatic, merely hinged, and closed under the impact. Wedhi seized Falkayn's hand and pressed something into the palm. Simultaneously, he caught his lips between his teeth. A signal for silence?

With a tingle along his spine, Falkayn nodded and stuffed the bit of paper into a pocket.

When he was alone, he opened the note, hunched over in case of spy eyes. The alphabet hadn't changed.

Be wary, star dweller. Morruchan Long-Ax is no friend. If you can arrange for one of your company to come tonight in secret to the house at the corner of Triau's Street and Victory Way which is marked by twined fylfots over the door, the truth shall be explained.

As darkness fell, the moon Neihevin rose full, Luna size and copper color, above eastward hills whose forests glistened with frost. Lythyr was already up, a small pale crescent. Rigel blazed in the heart of that constellation named the Spear Bearer.

Chee Lan turned from the viewscreen with a shiver and an unladylike phrase. 'But I am not equipped to do that,' said the ship's computer.

'The suggestion was addressed to my gods,' Chee answered.

She sat for a while, brooding on her wrongs. Ta-chih-chien-pih – O_2 Eridani A II or Cynthia to humans – felt even more distant than it was, warm ruddy sunlight and rustling leaves around treetop homes lost in time as well as space. Not only the cold outside daunted her. Those Merseians were so bloody *big*!

She herself was no larger than a medium-sized dog, though the bush of her tail added a good deal. Her arms, almost as long as her legs, ended in delicate six-fingered hands. White fur fluffed about her, save where it made a bluish mask across the green eyes and round, blunt-muzzled face. Seeing her for the first time, human females were apt to call her darling.

She bristled. Ears, whiskers, and hair stood erect. What was she – descendant of carnivores who chased their prey in five-meter leaps from branch to branch, xeno-biologist by training, trade pioneer by choice, and pistol champion because she liked to shoot guns – what was she doing, feeling so much as respect for a gaggle of slew-footed bald barbarians? Mainly she was irritated. While standing by aboard the ship, she'd hoped to complete her latest piece of sculpture. Instead, she must hustle into that pustulent excuse for weather, and skulk through a stone garbage dump that its perpetrators called a city, and hear some yokel drone on for hours about some squabble between drunken cockroaches which he thought was politics . . . and pretend to take the whole farce seriously!

A narcotic cigarette soothed her, however ferocious the puffs in which she consumed it. 'I guess the matter is important, at that,' she murmured. 'Fat commissions for me if the project succeeds.'

'My programming is to the effect that our primary objective is humanitarian,' said the computer. 'Though I cannot find that concept in my data storage.'

'Never mind, Muddlehead,' Chee replied. Her mood had turned benign. 'If you want to know, it relates to those constraints you have filed under Law and Ethics. But no concern of ours, this trip. Oh, the bleeding hearts do quack about Rescuing a Promising Civilization, as if the galaxy didn't have too chaos many civilizations already. Well, if they want to foot the bill, it's their taxes. They'll have to work with the League, because the League has most of the ships, which it won't hire out for nothing. And the League has to start with us, because trade pioneers are supposed to be experts in making first contacts and we happened to be the sole such crew in reach. Which is our good luck, I suppose.'

She stubbed out her cigarette and busied herself with preparations. There was, for a fact, no alternative. She'd had to admit that, after a three-way radio conversation with her partners. (They didn't worry about eavesdroppers, when not a Merseian knew a word of Anglic.) Falkayn was stuck in what's-his-name's palace. Adzel was loose in the city, but he'd be the last one you'd pick for an undercover mission. Which left Chee Lan.

'Maintain contact with all three of us,' she ordered the ship. 'Record everything coming in tonight over my two-way. Don't stir without orders – in a galactic language – and don't respond to any native attempts at communication. Tell us at once whatever unusual you observe. If you haven't heard from any of us for twenty-four hours at a stretch, return to Catawrayannis and report.'

No answer being indicated, the computer made none.

Chee buckled on a gravity harness, a tool kit, and two guns, a stunner and a blaster. Over them she threw a black mantle, less for warmth than concealment. Dousing the lights, she had the personal lock open just long enough to let her through, jumped, and took to the air.

It bit her with chill. Flowing past, it felt liquid. An enormous silence dwelt beneath heaven; the hum of her grav was lost. Passing above the troopers who surrounded *Muddlin' Through* with armor and artillery – a sensible precaution from the native standpoint, she had to agree, sensibly labelled an honor guard – she saw the forlorn twinkle of campfires and heard a snatch of hoarse song. Then a hovercraft whirred near, big and black athwart the Milky Way, and she must change course to avoid being seen.

For a while she flew above snow-clad wilderness. On an unknown planet, you didn't land downtown if you could help it. Hills and woods gave way at length to a cultivated plain where the lights of villages huddled around tower-jagged castles. Merseia – this continent, at least – appeared to have retained feudalism even as it swung into an industrial age. Or had it?

Perhaps tonight she would find out.

The seacoast hove in view, and Ardaig. That city did not gleam with illumination and brawl with traffic as most Technic communities did. Yellow windows strewed its night, like fireflies trapped in a web of phosphorescent paving. The River Oiss gleamed dull where it poured through town and into the bay, on which there shone a double moonglade. No, triple; Wythna was rising now. A murmur of machines lifted skyward.

Chee dodged another aircraft and streaked down for the darkling Old Quarter. She landed behind a shuttered bazaar and sought the nearest alley. Crouched there, she peered forth. In this section, the streets were decked with a hardy turf which ice had blanketed, and lit by widely spaced lamps. A Merseian went past, riding a horned gwydh. His tail was draped back across the animal's rump; his cloak fluttered behind him to reveal a quilted jacket reinforced with glittering metal discs, and a rifle slanted over his shoulder.

No guardsman, surely; Chee had seen what the military wore, and Falkayn had transmitted pictures of Morruchan's household troops to her via a hand scanner. He had also passed on the information that those latter doubled as police. So why was a civilian going armed? It bespoke a degree of lawlessness that fitted ill with a technological society . . . unless that society was in more trouble than Morruchan had admitted. Chee made certain her own guns were loose in the holsters.

The clop-clop of hooves faded away. Chee stuck her head out of the alley and took bearings from street signs. Instead of words, they used colorful heraldic emblems. But the Survey people had compiled a good map of Ardaig, which Falkayn's gang had memorized. The Old Quarter ought not to have changed much. She loped off, seeking cover whenever she heard a rider or pedestrian approach. There weren't many.

This corner! Squinting through murk, she identified the symbol carved in the lintel of a lean gray house. Quickly, she ran up the stairs and rapped on the door. Her free hand rested on the stunner.

The door creaked open. Light streamed through. A Merseian stood silhouetted against it. He carried a pistol himself. His head moved back and forth, peering into the night. 'Here I am, thou idiot,' Chee muttered.

He looked down. A jerk went through his body. '*Hu-ya!* You are from the star ship?'

'Nay,' Chee sneered, 'I am come to inspect the plumbing.' She darted past him, into a wainscoted corridor. 'If thou wouldst preserve this chickling secrecy of thine, might one suggest that thou close yon portal?'

The Merseian did. He stood a moment, regarding her in the glow of an incandescent bulb overhead. 'I thought you would be ... different.'

'They were Terrans who first visited this world, but surely thou didst not think every race in the cosmos is formed to those ridiculous specifications. Now I've scant time to spare for whatever griping ye have here to do, so lead me to thine acher.'

The Merseian obeyed. His garments were about like ordinary street clothes, belted tunic and baggy trousers, but a certain precision in their cut – as well as blue-and-gold stripes and the double fylfot embroidered on the sleeves – indicated they were a livery. Or a uniform? Chee felt the second guess confirmed when she noted two others, similarly attired, standing armed in front of a door. They saluted her and let her through.

The room beyond was baronial. Radiant heating had been installed, but a fire also roared on the hearth. Chee paid scant attention to rich draperies and carven pillars. Her gaze went to the two who sat awaiting her.

One was scarfaced, athletic, his tailtip restlessly aflicker. His robe was blue and gold, and he carried a short ceremonial spear. At sight of her, he drew a quick breath. The Cynthian decided she'd better be polite. 'I hight Chee Lan, worthies, come from the interstellar expedition in response to your kind invitation.'

'*Khraich.*' The aristocrat recovered his poise and touched finger to brow. 'Be welcome. I am Dagla, called Quick-to-Anger, the Hand of the Vach Hallen. And my comrade: Olgor hu Freylin, his rank Warmaster in the Republic of Lafdigu, here in Ardaig as agent for his country.'

That being was middle-aged, plump, with skin more dark and features more flat than was common around the Wilwidh Ocean. His garb was foreign too, a sort of toga with metal threads woven into the purple cloth. And he was soft-spoken, imperturbable, quite without the harshness of these lands. He crossed his arms – gesture of greeting? – and said in accented Eriau:

'Great is the honor. Since the last visitors from your high civilization were confined largely to this region, perhaps you have no knowledge of mine. May I therefore say that Lafdigu lies in the southern hemisphere, occupying a goodly part of its continent. In those days we were unindustrialized, but now, one hopes, the situation has altered.'

'Nay, Warmaster, be sure our folk heard much about Lafdigu's venerable culture and regretted they had no time to learn therefrom.' Chee got more tactful the bigger the lies she told. Inwardly, she groaned: *Oh, no! We haven't troubles enough, there has to be international politicking too!*

A servant appeared with a cut-crystal decanter and goblets. 'I trust that your race, like the Terran, can partake of Merseian refreshment?' Dagla said.

'Indeed,' Chee replied. ' 'Tis necessary that they who voyage together use the same stuffs. I thank the Hand.'

'But we had not looked for, *hurgh*, a guest your size,' Olgor said. 'Perhaps a smaller glass? The wine is potent.'

'This is excellent.' Chee hopped onto a low table, squatted, and raised her goblet two-handed. 'Galactic custom is that we drink to the health of friends. To yours, then, worthies.' She took a long draught. The fact that alcohol does not affect the Cynthian brain was one she had often found it advantageous to keep silent about.

Dagla tossed off a yet larger amount, took a turn around the room, and growled: 'Enough formalities, by your leave, Shipmaster.' She discarded her cloak. 'Shipmistress?' He gulped. His society had a kitchen-church-and-kids attitude toward females. 'We – *kh-h-h* – we've grave matters to discuss.'

'The Hand is too abrupt with our noble guest,' Olgor chided.

'Nay, time is short,' Chee said. 'And clearly the business hath great weight, sith ye went to the length of suborning a servant in Morruchan's very stronghold.'

Dagla grinned. 'I planted Wedhi there eight years ago. He's a good voice-tube.'

'No doubt the Hand of the Vach Hallen hath surety of all his own servitors?' Chee purred.

Dagla frowned. Olgor's lips twitched upward.

'Chances must be taken.' Dagla made a chopping gesture. 'All we know is what was learned from your first radio communications, which said little. Morruchan was quick to isolate you. His hope is plainly to let you hear no more of the truth than he wants. To use you! Here, in this house, we may speak frankly with each other.'

As frankly as you two klongs choose, Chee thought. 'I listen with care,' she said.

Piece by piece, between Dagla and Olgor, the story emerged. It sounded reasonable, as far as it went.

When the Survey team arrived, the Wilwidh culture stood on the brink of a machine age. The scientific method had been invented. There was a heliocentric astronomy, a post-Newtonian, pre-Maxwellian physics, a dawning chemistry, a well-developed taxonomy, some speculations about evolution. Steam engines were at work on the first railroads. But political power was fragmented among the Vachs. The scientists, the engineers, the teachers were each under the patronage of one or another Hand.

The visitors from space had too much sense of responsibility to pass on significant practical information. It wouldn't have done a great deal of good anyway. How do you make transistors, for instance, before you can refine ultrapure semimetals? And why should you want to, when you don't yet have electronics? But the humans had given theoretical and experimental science a boost by what they related – above all, by the simple and tremendous fact of their presence.

And then they left.

A fierce, proud people had their noses rubbed in their own insignificance. Chee guessed that here lay the root of most of the social upheaval which followed. And belike a more urgent motive than curiosity or profit began to drive the scientists: the desire, the need to catch up, to bring Merseia in one leap onto the galactic scene.

The Vachs had shrewdly ridden the wave. Piecemeal they shelved their quarrels, formed a loose confederation, met the new problems well enough that no movement arose to strip them of their privileges. But rivalry persisted, and cross purposes, and often a reactionary spirit, a harking back to olden days when the young were properly respectful of the God and their elders.

And meanwhile modernization spread across the planet. A country which did not keep pace soon found itself under foreign domination. Lafdigu had succeeded best. Chee got a distinct impression that the Republic was actually a hobnail-booted dictatorship. Its own imperial ambitions clashed with those of the Hands. Nuclear war was averted on the ground, but space battles had erupted from time to time, horribly and inconclusively.

'So here we are,' Dagla said. 'Largest, most powerful, the Vach Dathyr speak loudest in this realm. But others press upon them, Hallen, Ynvory, Rueth, yes, even landless Urdiolch. You can see what it would mean if any one of them obtained your exclusive services.'

Olgor nodded. 'Among other things,' he said, 'Morruchan Long-Ax would like to contrive that my country is ignored. We are in the southern hemisphere. We will get the worst of the supernova blast. If unprotected, we will be removed from his equations.'

'In whole truth, Shipmistress,' Dagla added, 'I don't believe Morruchan wants your help. *Khraich*, yes, a minimum, to forestall utter collapse. But he has long ranted against the modern world and its ways. He'd not be sorry to see industrial civilization reduced so small that full-plumed feudalism returns.'

'How shall he prevent us from doing our work?' Chee asked. 'Surely he is not fool enough to kill us. Others will follow.'

'He'll bet the knucklebones as they fall,' Dagla said. 'At the very least, he'll try to keep his position – that you work through him and get most of your information from his sources – and use it to increase his power. At the expense of every other party!'

'We could predict it even in Lafdigu, when first we heard of your coming,' Olgor said. 'The Strategic College dispatched me here to make what alliances I can. Several Hands are not unwilling to see my country continue as a force in the world, as the price for our help in diminishing their closer neighbors.'

Chee said slowly: 'Meseems ye make no few assumptions about us, on scant knowledge.'

'Shipmistress,' said Olgor, 'civilized Merseia has had two centuries to study each word, each picture, each legend about your people. Some believe you akin to gods – or demons – yes, whole cults have flowered from the expectation of your return, and I do not venture to guess what they will do now that you are come. But there have also been cooler minds; and that first expedition was honest in what it told, was it not?

'Hence: the most reasonable postulate is that none of the starfaring races have mental powers we do not. They simply have longer histories. And as we came to know how many the stars are, we saw how thinly your civilization must be spread among them. You will not expend any enormous effort on us, in terms of your own economy. You cannot. You have too much else to do. Nor have you time to learn everything about Merseia and decide every detail of what you will effect. The supernova will flame in our skies in less than three years. You must cooperate with whatever authorities you find, and take their words for what the crucial things are to save and what others must be abandoned. Is this not truth?'

Chee weighed her answer. 'To a certain degree,' she said carefully, 'ye have right.'

'Morruchan knows this,' Dagla said. 'He'll use the knowledge as best he can.' He leaned forward, towering above her. 'For our part, we will not tolerate it. Better the world go down in ruin, to be rebuilt by us, than that the Vach Dathyr engulf what our ancestors wrought. No planetwide effort can succeed without the help of a majority. Unless we get a full voice in what decisions are made, we'll fight.'

'Hand, Hand,' reproved Olgor.

'Nay, I take no offense,' Chee said. 'Rather, I give thanks for so plain a warning. Ye will understand, we bear ill will toward none on Merseia, and have no partisanship – ' *in your wretched little jockeyings.* 'If ye have prepared a document stating your position, gladly will we ponder on the same.'

Olgor opened a casket and took out a sheaf of papers bound in something like snakeskin. 'This was hastily written,' he apologized. 'At another date we would like to give you a fuller account.'

' 'Twill serve for the nonce.' Chee wondered if she should stay a while. No doubt she could learn something further. But chaos, how much propaganda she'd have to strain out of what she heard! Also, she'd now been diplomatic as long as anyone could expect. Hadn't she?

They could call the ship directly, she told them. If Morruchan tried to jam the airwaves, she'd jam him, into an unlikely posture. Olgor looked shocked. Dagla objected to communication which could be monitored. Chee sighed. 'Well, then, invite us hither for a private talk,' she said. 'Will Morruchan attack you for that?'

'No . . . I suppose not . . . but he'll get some idea of what we know and what we're doing.'

'My belief was,' said Chee in her smoothest voice, 'that the Hand of the Vach Hallen wished naught save an end to these intrigues and selfishnesses, an openness in which Merseians might strive together for the common welfare.'

She had never cherished any such silly notion, but Dagla couldn't very well admit that his chief concern was to get his own relatives on top of everybody else. He made wistful noises about a transmitter which could not be detected by Merseian equipment. Surely the galactics had one? They did, but Chee wasn't about to pass on stuff with that kind of potentialities. She expressed regrets – nothing had been brought along – so sorry – goodnight, Hand, goodnight, Warmaster.

The guard who had let her in escorted her to the front

door. She wondered why her hosts didn't. Caution, or just a different set of mores? Well, no matter. Back to the ship. She ran down the frosty street, looking for an alley from which her takeoff wouldn't be noticed. Someone might get trigger happy.

An entrance gaped between two houses. She darted into darkness. A body fell upon her. Other arms clasped tight, pinioning. She yelled. A light gleamed briefly, a sack was thrust over her head, she inhaled a sweet-sick odor and whirled from her senses.

Adzel still wasn't sure what was happening to him, or how it had begun. There he'd been, minding his own business, and suddenly he was the featured speaker at a prayer meeting. If that was what it was.

He cleared his throat. 'My friends,' he said.

A roar went through the hall. Faces and faces and faces stared at the rostrum which he filled with his four and a half meters of length. A thousand Merseians must be present: clients, commoners, city proletariat, drably clad for the most part. Many were female; the lower classes didn't segregate sexes as rigidly as the upper. Their odors made the air thick and musky. Being in a new part of Ardaig, the hall was built plain. But its proportions, the contrasting hues of paneling, the symbols painted in scarlet across the walls, reminded Adzel he was on a foreign planet.

He took advantage of the interruption to lift the transceiver hung around his neck up to his snout and mutter plaintively, 'David, what *shall* I tell them?'

'Be benevolent and noncommittal,' Falkayn's voice advised. 'I don't think mine host likes this one bit.'

The Wodenite glanced over the seething crowd, to the entrance. Three of Morruchan's household guards stood by the door and glowered.

He didn't worry about physical attack. Quite apart from having the ship for a backup, he was too formidable himself: a thousand-kilo centauroid, his natural armor-plate shining green above and gold below, his spine more impressively ridged than any Merseian's. His ears were not soft cartilage but bony, a similar shelf protected his eyes, his rather crocodilian face opened on an alarming array of fangs. Thus he had been the logical member of the team to wander around the city today, gathering impressions. Morruchan's arguments against this had been politely overruled. 'Fear no trouble, Hand,' Falkayn said truthfully. 'Adzel never seeketh any out. He is a Buddhist, a lover of peace who can well afford tolerance anent the behavior of others.'

By the same token, though, he had not been able to refuse the importunities of the crowd which finally cornered him.

'Have you got word from Chee?' he asked.

'Nothing yet,' Falkayn said. 'Muddlehead's monitoring, of course. I imagine she'll contact us tomorrow. Now don't you interrupt me either, I'm in the middle of an interminable official banquet.'

Adzel raised his arms for silence, but here that gesture was an encouragement for more shouts. He changed position, his hooves clattering on the platform, and his tail knocked over a floor candelabrum. 'Oh, I'm sorry,' he exclaimed. A red-robed Merseian named Gryf, the chief nut of this organization – Star Believers, was that what they called themselves? – picked the thing up and managed to silence the house.

'My friends,' Adzel tried again. 'Er . . . my friends. I am, er, deeply appreciative of the honor ye do me in asking for some few words.' He tried to remember the political speeches he had heard while a student on Earth. 'In the great fraternity of intelligent races throughout

67

the universe, surely Merseia hath a majestic part to fulfill.'

'Show us – show us the way!' howled from the floor. 'The way, the truth, the long road futureward!'

'Ah . . . yes. With pleasure.' Adzel turned to Gryf. 'But perchance first your, er, glorious leader should explain to me the purposes of this – this – ' What was the word for 'club'? Or did he want 'church'?

Mainly he wanted information.

'Why, the noble galactic jests,' Gryf said in ecstasy. 'You know we are those who have waited, living by the precepts the galactics taught, in loyal expectation of their return which they promised us. We are your chosen instrument for the deliverance of Merseia from its ills. Use us!'

Adzel was a planetologist by profession, but his large bump of curiosity had led him to study in other fields. His mind shuffled through books he had read, societies he had visited . . . yes, he identified the pattern. These were cultists, who'd attached a quasi-religious significance to what had actually been quite a casual stopover. Oh, the jewel in the lotus! What kind of mess had ensued?'

He had to find out.

'That's, ah, very fine,' he said. 'Very fine indeed. Ah . . . how many do ye number?'

'More than two million, Protector, in twenty different nations. Some high ones are among us, yes, the Heir of the Vach Isthyr. But most belong to the virtuous poor. Had they all known the Protector was to walk forth this day – Well, they'll come as fast as may be, to hear your bidding.'

An influx like that could make the pot boil over, Adzel foresaw. Ardaig had been restless enough as he quested through its streets. And what little had been learned about basic Merseian instincts, by the Survey psychologists, suggested they were a combative species. Mass

68

hysteria could take ugly forms.

'No!' the Wodenite cried. The volume nearly blew Gryf off the podium. Adzel moderated his tone. 'Let them stay home. Calm, patience, carrying out one's daily round of duties, those are the galactic virtues.'

Try telling that to a merchant adventurer! Adzel checked himself. 'I fear we have no miracles to offer.'

He was about to say that the word he carried was of blood, sweat, and tears. But no. When you dealt with a people whose reactions you couldn't predict, such news must be released with care. Falkayn's first radio communications had been guarded, on precisely that account.

'This is clear,' Gryf said. He was not stupid, or even crazy, except in his beliefs. 'We must ourselves release ourselves from our oppressors. Tell us how to begin.'

Adzel saw Morruchan's troopers grip their rifles tight. *We're expected to start some kind of social revolution?* he thought wildly. *But we can't! It's not our business. Our business is to save your lives, and for that we must not weaken but strengthen whatever authority can work with us, and any revolution will be slow to mature, a consequence of technology – Dare I tell them this tonight?*

Pedantry might soothe them, if only by boring them to sleep. 'Among those sophonts who need a government,' Adzel said, 'the basic requirement for a government which is to function well is that it be legitimate, and the basic problem of any political innovator is how to continue, or else establish anew, a sound basis for that legitimacy. Thus newcomers like mineself cannot – '

He was interrupted (later he was tempted to say 'rescued') by a noise outside. It grew louder, a harsh chant, the clatter of feet on pavement. Females in the audience wailed. Males snarled and moved toward the door. Gryf sprang from the platform, down to what Adzel identified as a telecom, and activated the scanner. It showed the street, and an armed mob. High over them, against snow-laden roofs and night sky, flapped a yellow banner.

'Demonists!' Gryf groaned. 'I was afraid of this.'

Adzel joined him. 'Who be they?'

'A lunatic sect. They imagine you galactics mean, have meant from the first, to corrupt us to our destruction . . . I was prepared, though. See.' From alleys and doorways moved close-ranked knots of husky males. They carried weapons.

A trooper snapped words into the microphone of a walkie-talkie. Sending for help, no doubt, to quell the oncoming riot. Adzel returned to the rostrum and filled the hall with his pleas that everyone remain inside.

He might have succeeded, by reverberation if not reason. But his own transceiver awoke with Falkayn's voice: 'Get here at once! Chee's been nabbed!'

'What? Who did it? Why?' The racket around became of scant importance.

'I don't know. Muddlehead just alerted me. She'd left this place she was at. Muddlehead received a yell, sounds of scuffling, then no more from her. I'm sending him aloft, to try and track her by the carrier wave. He says the source is moving. You move too, back to Afon.'

Adzel did. He took part of the wall with him.

Korych rose through winter mists that turned gold as they smoked past city towers and above the river. Kettledrums rolled their ritual from Eidh Hill. Shutters came down off windows and doors, market circles began to fill, noise lifted out of a hundred small workshops. Distantly, but deeper and more portentous, sounded the buzz of traffic and power from the new quarters, hoot of ships on the bay, whine of jets overhead, thunder of rockets as a craft left the spaceport for the moon Seith.

70

Morruchan Long-Ax switched off the lights in his confidence chamber. Dawnglow streamed pale through glass, picking out the haggardness of faces. 'I am weary,' he said, 'and we are on a barren trail.'

'Hand,' said Falkayn, 'it had better not be. Here we stay until we have reached some decision.'

Morruchan and Dagla glared. Olgor grew expressionless. They were none of them accustomed to being addressed thus. Falkayn gave them stare for stare, and Adzel lifted his head from where he lay coiled on the floor. The Merseians slumped back onto their tails.

'Your whole world may be at stake, worthies,' Falkayn said. 'My people will not wish to spend time and treasure, aye, some lives, if they look for such ungrateful treatment.'

He picked up the harness and kit which lay on Morruchan's desk and hefted them. Guided by Muddlehead, searchers from his household had found the apparatus in a ditch outside town and brought it here several hours ago. Clearly Chee's kidnappers had suspected a signal was being emitted. The things felt pitifully light in his hand.

'What more can be said?' Olgor argued. 'We have each voiced a suspicion that one of the others engineered the deed to gain a lever for himself. Or yet a different Vach, or another nation, may have done it; or the Demonists; or even the Star Believers, for some twisted reason.' He turned to Dagla. 'Are you certain you have no inkling who that servant of yours may have been working for?'

'I told you before, no,' said the Hallen chief. 'It's not our way in this country to pry into lives. I know only that Dwyr entered my service a few years ago, and gave satisfaction, and now has also vanished. So I presume he was a spy for someone else, and told his masters of a chance to seize a galactic. A telecom call would be easy to make, and they needed only to cover the few possible routes she could take on leaving me.'

'In sum,' Morruchan declared, 'he acted just like your spy who betrayed my doings to you.'

'Enough, worthies,' Falkayn sighed. 'Too stinking often this night have we tracked the same ground. Perchance investigation will give some clues to this Dwyr, whence he came and so forth. But such taketh time. We must needs look into every possibility at once. Including your very selves. Best ye perform a mutual checking.'

'And who shall do the like for you?' Morruchan asked. 'What meaneth the Hand?'

'This might be a trick of your own.'

Falkayn clutched his hair. 'For what conceivable reason?' He wanted to say more, but relations were strained already.

'How should I know?' Morruchan retorted. 'You are unknowns. You *say* you have no imperial designs here, but your agents have met with rivals of mine, with a cult whose main hope is to upset the order of things – and with how many else? The Gethfennu?'

'Would the Hand be so gracious as to explain to me who those are?' said Adzel in an oil-on-the-waves voice.

'We described them already,' Dagla answered.

'Then 'twas whilst I was out, Hand, directing our ship in its search and subsequent return to base. Indulge a humble fool's request, I beg you.'

The idea of someone equipped like Adzel calling himself a humble fool took the Merseians so much aback that they forgot to stay angry. Falkayn added: 'I'd not mind hearing about them again. Never suspected I their existence erenow.'

'They are the criminal syndicate, spread across the world and on into space,' Morruchan said. 'Thieves, assassins, harlots, tricksters, corrupters of all good.'

He went on, while Falkayn analyzed his words. No doubt the Gethfennu were a bad influence. But Morruchan was too prejudiced, and had too little historical sense, to see why they flourished. The industrial revolution had shaken foundation stones loose from society. Workers flocking to the cities found themselves cut off from the old feudal restrictions ... and securities. Cultural and material impoverishment breed lawlessness. Yet the baronial tradition survived, in a distorted form; gangs were soon gathered into a network which offered members protection and purpose as well as loot.

The underground kingdom of the Gethfennu could not be destroyed by Vachs and nations divided against each other. It fought back too effectively, with money and influence more often than with violence. And, to be sure, it provided some safety valve. A commoner who went to one of its gambling dens or joyhouses might get fleeced, but he would not plot insurrection.

So a tacit compromise was reached, the kind that many planets have known, Earth not least among them. Racketeering and vice were held to a tolerable level, confined to certain areas and certain classes, by the gang lords. Murder, robbery, and shakedown did not touch the aristocratic palace or the high financial office. Bribery did, in some countries, and thereby the Gethfennu was strengthened.

Of late, its tentacles had stretched beyond these skies. It brought into established interplanetary enterprises. And then there was Ronruad, the next planet out. Except for scientific research, it had scant intrinsic value, but bases upon it were of so great strategic importance that they had occasioned wars. Hence the last general peace treaty had neutralized it, placed it outside any jurisdiction. Soon afterward, the Gethfennu took advantage of this by building a colony there, where anything went. A spaceship line, under the syndicate's open-secret control, offered passenger service. Luridor became the foremost town for respectable Merseians to go in search of unrestrained, if expensive fun. It also became a hatchery of trouble, and Falkayn could understand why Morruchan didn't want it protected against the supernova.

Neither, he found, did Dagla. Probably few if any Hands did. Olgor was less emphatic, but agreed that, at best, Ronruad should get a very low priority.

'The Gethfennu may, then, have seized Chee Lan for ransom?' Adzel said.

'Perhaps,' Dagla said. 'Though the ransom may be that you galactics help them. If they've infiltrated Hand Morruchan's service too, they could know what the situation is.'

'In that case,' Falkayn objected, 'they are scarcely so naive as to think – '

'I will investigate,' Morruchan promised. 'I may make direct inquiry. But channels of communication with the Gethfennu masters are devious, therefore slow.'

'In any event,' Falkayn said bleakly, 'Adzel and I do not propose to leave our partner in the grip of criminals – for years, after which they may cut her throat.'

'You do not know they have her,' Olgor reminded him.

'True. Yet may we prowl somewhat through space, out toward their colony. For little can we do on Merseia, where our knowledge is scant. Here must ye search, worthies, and contrive that all others search with you.'

The command seemed to break Morruchan's thin-stretched patience. 'Do you imagine we've nothing better to do than hunt for one creature? We, who steer millions?'

Falkayn lost his temper likewise. 'If ye wish to keep on doing thus, best ye make the finding of Chee Lan your foremost concern!'

'Gently, gently,' Olgor said. 'We are so tired that we

are turning on allies. And that is not well.' He laid a hand on Falkayn's shoulder. 'Galactic,' he said, 'surely you can understand that organizing a systemwide hunt, in a world as diverse as ours, is a greater task than the hunt itself. Why, no few leaders of nations, tribes, clans, factions will not believe the truth if they are told. Proving it to them will require diplomatic skill. Then there are others whose main interest will be to see if they cannot somehow maneuver this affair to give them an advantage over us. And yet others hope you do go away and never return; I do not speak merely of the Demonists.'

'If Chee be not returned safely,' Falkayn said, 'those last may well get their wish.'

Olgor smiled. The expression went no deeper than his lips. 'Galactic,' he murmured, 'let us not play word games. Your scientists stand to win knowledge and prestige here, your merchants a profit. They will not allow an unfortunate incident, caused by a few Merseians and affecting only one of their fold . . . they will not let that come between them and their objectives. Will they?'

Falkayn looked into the ebony eyes. His own were the first to drop. Nausea caught at his gullet. The Warmaster of Lafdigu had identified his bluff and called it.

Oh, no doubt these who confronted him would mount some kind of search. If nothing else, they'd be anxious to learn what outfit had infiltrated agents onto their staffs, and to what extent. No doubt, also, various other Merseians would cooperate. But the investigation would be ill-coordinated and lackadaisical. It would hardly succeed against beings as wily as those who captured Chee Lan.

These three here – nigh the whole of Merseia – just didn't give a damn about her.

She awoke in a cell.

It was less than three meters long, half that in width

and height: windowless, doorless, comfortless. A coat of paint did not hide the basic construction, which was of large blocks. Their unresponsiveness to her fist-pounding suggested a high density. Brackets were bolted into the walls, to hold equipment of different sorts in place. Despite non-Technic design, Chee recognized a glowlamp, a thermostated air renewer, a waste unit, an acceleration couch ... space gear, by Cosmos!

No sound, no vibration other than the faint whirr of the air unit's fan, reached her. The walls were altogether blank. After a while, they seemed to move closer. She chattered obscenities at them.

But she came near weeping with relief when one block slid aside. A Merseian face looked in. Behind was polished metal. Rumble, clangor, shouted commands resounded through what must be a spaceship's hull, from what must be a spaceport outside.

'Are you well?' asked the Merseian. He looked still tougher than average, but he was trying for courtesy, and he wore a neat tunic with insignia of rank.

Chee debated whether to make a jump, claw his eyes out, and bolt for freedom. No, not a chance. But neither was she going to embrace him. 'Quite well, I thank thee,' she snarled, 'if thou'lt set aside trifles such as that thy heart-rotten varlets have beaten and gassed me, and I am athirst and anhungered. For this outrage, methinks I'll summon my mates to blow thy pesthole of a planet from the universe it defileth.'

The Merseian laughed. 'You can't be too sick, with that kind of spirit. Here are food and water.' He passed her some containers. 'We blast off soon for a voyage of a few days. If I can supply you with anything safe, I will.'

'Where are we bound? Who art thou? What meaneth –'

'*Hurh*, little one, I'm not going to leave this smuggle-hole open very long, for any spillmouth to notice. Tell me this instant what you want, so I can try to have it sent from the city.'

Later Chee swore at herself, more picturesquely than she had ever cursed even Adzel. Had she specified the right things, they might have been a clue for her partners. But she was too foggy in the head, too dazed by events. Automatically, she asked for books and films which might help her understand the Merseian situation better. And a grammar text, she added in haste. She was tired of sounding like a local Shakespeare. The Merseian nodded and pushed the block back in place. She heard a faint click. Doubtless a tongue-and-groove lock, operated by a magnetic key.

The rations were revivifying. Before long, Chee felt in shape to make deductions. She was evidently in a secret compartment, built into the wall of a radiation shelter.

Merseian interplanetary vessels ran on a thermo-nuclear-powered ion drive. Those which made landings – ferries tending the big ships, or special jobs such as this presumably was – set down in deep silos and departed from them, so that electromagnetic fields could contain the blast and neutralize it before it poisoned the neigh-borhood. And each craft carried a blockhouse for crew and passengers to huddle in, should they get caught by a solar storm. Altogether, the engineering was superb. Too bad it would go by the board as soon as gravity drive and force screens became available.

A few days, at one Merseian gee: hm, that meant an adjacent planet. Not recalling the present positions, Chee wasn't sure which. A lot of space traffic moved in the Korychan System, as instruments had shown while *Muddlin' Through* approached. From a distance, in magniscreens, she had observed some of the fleet, capa-cious cargo vessels and sleek naval units.

Her captor returned with the materials she had requested and a warning to strap in for blastoff. He introduced himself genially as Iriad the Wayfarer, in charge of this dispatch boat.

'Who are thou working for?' Chee demanded.

He hesitated, then shrugged. 'The Gethfennu.' The block glided back to imprison her.

Lift was nothing like the easy upward floating of a galactic ship. Acceleration rammed Chee down into her couch and sat on her chest. Thunder shuddered through the very blockhouse. Eternal minutes passed before the pressure slacked off and the boat fell into steady running.

After that, for a timeless time, Chee had nothing to do but study. The officers brought her rations. They were a mixed lot, from every part of Merseia; some did not speak Eriau, and none had much to say to her. She considered tinkering her life support apparatus into a weapon, but without tools the prospect was hopeless. So for amusement she elaborated the things she would like to do to Iriad, come the day. Her partners would have flinched.

Once her stomach, the only clock she had, told her she was far overdue for a meal. When finally her cell was opened, she leaped forward in a whirlwind of abuse. Iriad stepped back and raised a pistol. Chee stopped and said: 'Well, what happened? Hadn't my swill gotten moldly enough?'

Iriad looked shaken. 'We were boarded,' he said low.

'How's that?' Acceleration had never varied.

'By . . . your people. They laid alongside, matching our vector as easily as one runner might pace another. I did not know what armament they had, so – He who came aboard was a dragon.'

Chee beat her fists on the shelter deck. Oh, no, no, no! Adzel had passed within meters of her, and never suspected . . . the big, ugly, vacuum-skulled bumblemaker!

Iriad straightened. 'But Haguan warned me it might

happen,' he said with a return of self-confidence. 'We know somewhat about smuggling. And you are not gods, you galactics.'

'Where did they go?'

'Away. To inspect other vessels. Let them.'

'Do you seriously hope to keep me hidden for long?'

'Ronruad is full of Haguan's boltholes.' Iriad gave her her lunch, collected the empty containers, and departed.

He came back several meals later, to supervise her transferral from the cell to a packing crate. Under guns, Chee obeyed his instructions. She was strapped into padding, alongside an air unit, and left in darkness. There followed hours of maneuver, landing, waiting, being unloaded and trucked to some destination.

Finally the box was opened. Chee emerged slowly. Weight was less than half a standard gee, but her muscles were cramped. A pair of workers bore the crate away. Guards stayed behind, with a Merseian who claimed to be a medic. The checkup he gave her was expert and sophisticated enough to bear him out. He said she should rest a while, and they left her alone.

Her suite was interior but luxurious. The food brought her was excellent. She curled in bed and told herself to sleep.

Eventually she was taken down a long, panelled corridor and up a spiral ramp to meet him who had ordered her caught.

He squatted behind a desk of dark, polished wood that looked a hectare in area. Thick white fur carpeted the room and muffled footsteps. Pictures glowed, music sighed, incense sweetened the air. Windows gave a view outside; this part of the warren projected aboveground. Chee saw ruddy sand, strange wild shrubbery, a dust storm walking across a gaunt range of hills and crowned with ice crystals. Korych stood near the horizon, shrunken, but fierce through the tenuous atmosphere. A few stars also shone in that purple sky. Chee recognized Valenderay, and shivered a little. So bright and steady it looked; and yet, at this moment, death was riding from it on the wings of light.

'Greeting, galactic.' The Eriau was accented differently from Olgor's. 'I am Haguan Eluatz. Your name, I gather, is Chee Lan.'

She arched her back, bottled her tail, and spat. But she felt very helpless. The Merseian was huge, with a belly that bulged forward his embroidered robe. He was not of the Wilwidh stock, his skin was shiny black and heavily scaled, his eyes almond-shaped, his nose a scimitar.

One ring-glittering hand made a gesture. Chee's guards slapped tails to ankles and left. The door closed behind them. But a pistol lay on Haguan's desk, next to an intercom.

He smiled. 'Be not afraid. No harm is intended you. We regret the indignities you have suffered and will try to make amends. Sheer necessity forced us to act.'

'The necessity for suicide?' Chee snorted.

'For survival. Now why don't you make yourself comfortable on yonder couch? We have talk to forge, we two. I can send for whatever refreshment you desire. Some arthberry wine, perhaps?'

Chee shook her head, but did jump onto the seat. 'Suppose you explain your abominable behavior,' she said.

'Gladly.' Haguan shifted the weight on his tail. 'You may not know what the Gethfennu is. It came into being after the first galactics had departed. But by now – ' He continued for a while. When he spoke of a systemwide syndicate, controlling millions of lives and uncounted wealth, strong enough to build its own city on this planet and clever enough to play its enemies off against each other so that none dared attack that colony: he was scarcely lying. Everything that Chee had seen confirmed it.

'Are we in this town of yours now?' she asked.

'No. Elsewhere on Ronruad. Best I not be specific. I have too much respect for your cleverness.'

'And I have none for yours.'

'*Khraich?* You must. I think we operated quite smoothly, and on such short notice. Of course, an organization like ours must always be prepared for anything. And we have been on special alert ever since your arrival. What little we have learned – ' Haguan's gaze went to the white point of Valenderay and lingered. 'That star, it is going to explode. True?'

'Yes. Your civilization will be scrubbed out unless – '

'I know, I know. We have scientists in our pay.' Haguan leaned forward. 'The assorted governments on Merseia see this as a millennial chance to rid themselves of the troublesome Gethfennu. We need only be denied help in saving our colony, our shipping, our properties on the home planet and elsewhere. Then we are finished. I expect you galactics would agree to this. Since not everything can be shielded in time, why not include us in that which is to be abandoned? You stand for some kind of law and order too, I suppose.'

Chee nodded. In their mask of dark fur, her eyes smoldered emerald. Haguan had guessed shrewdly. The League didn't much care who it dealt with, but the solid citizens whose taxes were to finance the majority of the rescue operations did.

'So to win our friendship, you take me by force,' she sneered half-heartedly.

'What had we to lose? We might have conferred with you, pleaded our cause, but would that have wrought good for us?'

6

'Suppose my partners recommend that no help be given your whole coprophagous Merseian race.'

'Why, then the collapse comes,' Haguan said with chilling calm, 'and the Gethfennu has a better chance than most organizations of improving its relative position. But I doubt that any such recommendation will be made, or that your overlords would heed it if it were.

'So we need a coin to buy technical assistance. You.'

Chee's whiskers twitched in a smile of sorts. 'I'm scarcely that big a hostage.'

'Probably not,' Haguan agreed. 'But you are a source of information.'

The Cynthian's fur stood on end with alarm. 'Do you have some skewbrained notion that I can tell you how to do everything for yourself? I'm not even an engineer!'

'Understood. But surely you know your way about in your own civilization. You know what the engineers can and cannot do. More important, you know the planets, the different races and cultures upon them, the mores, the laws, the needs. You can tell us what to expect. You can help us get interstellar ships – hijacking under your advice should succeed, being unlooked for – and show us how to pilot them, and put us in touch with someone who, for pay, will come to our aid.'

'If you suppose for a moment that the Polesotechnic League would tolerate – '

Teeth flashed white in Haguan's face. 'Perhaps it won't, perhaps it will. With so many stars, the diversity of peoples and interests is surely inconceivable. The Gethfennu is skilled in stirring up competition among others. What information you supply will tell us how, in this particular case. I don't really visualize your League, whatever it is, fighting a war – at a time when every resource must be devoted to saving Merseia – to prevent someone else rescuing us.'

He spread his hands. 'Or possibly we'll find a different approach,' he finished. 'It depends on what you tell and suggest.'

'How do you know you can trust me?'

Haguan said like iron: 'We judge the soil by what crops it bears. If we fail, if we see the Gethfennu doomed, we can still enforce our policy regarding traitors. Would you care to visit my punishment facilities? They are quite extensive. Even though you are of a new species, I think we could keep you alive and aware for many days.'

Silence dwelt a while in that room. Korych slipped under the horizon. Instantly the sky was black, strewn with the legions of the stars, beautiful and uncaring.

Haguan switched on a light, to drive away that too enormous vision. 'If you save us, however,' he said, 'you will go free with a very good reward.'

'But – ' Chee looked sickly into sterile years ahead of her. And the betrayal of friends, and scorn if ever she returned, a lifetime's exile. 'You'll keep me till then?'

'Of course.'

No success. No ghost of a clue. She was gone into an emptiness less fathomable than the spaces which gaped around their ship.

They had striven, Falkayn and Adzel. They had walked into Luridor itself, the sin-bright city on Ronruad, while the ship hovered overhead and showed with a single, rock-fusing flash of energy guns what power menaced the world. They had ransacked, threatened, bribed, beseeched. Sometimes terror met them, sometimes the inborn arrogance of Merseia's lords. But nowhere and never had anyone so much as hinted he knew who held Chee Lan or where.

Falkayn ran a hand through uncombed yellow locks. His eyes stood bloodshot in a sunken countenance. 'I still think we should've taken that casino boss aboard and worked him over.'

'No,' said Adzel. 'Apart from the morality of the matter, I feel sure that everyone who has any information is hidden away. That precaution is elementary. We're not even certain the outlaw regime is responsible.'

'Yeh. Could be Morruchan, Dagla, Olgor, or colleagues of theirs acting unbeknownst to them, or any of a hundred other governments, or some gang of fanatics, or – Oh, *Judas*!'

Falkayn looked at the after viewscreen. Ronruad's tawny-red crescent was dwindling swiftly among the constellations, as the ship drove at full acceleration back toward Merseia. It was a dwarf planet, an ocherous pebble that would not make a decent splash if it fell into one of the gas giants. But the least of planets is still a world: mountains, plains, valleys, arroyos, caves, waters, square kilometers by the millions, too vast and varied for any mind to grasp. And Merseia was bigger yet; and there were others, and moons, asteroids, space itself.

Chee's captors need but move her around occasionally, and the odds against a fleetful of League detectives finding her would climb for infinity.

'The Merseians themselves are bound to have some notion where to look, what to do, who to put pressure on,' he mumbled for the hundredth time. 'We don't know the ins and outs. Nobody from our cultures ever will – five billion years of planetary existence to catch up with! We've got to get the Merseians busy. I mean really busy.'

'They have their own work to do,' Adzel said.

Falkayn expressed himself at pungent length on the value of their work. 'How about those enthusiasts?' he wondered when he had calmed down a trifle. 'The outfit you were talking to.'

'Yes, the Star Believers should be loyal allies,' Adzel

said. 'But most of them are poor and, ah, unrealistic. I hardly expect them to be of help. Indeed, I fear they will complicate our problem by starting pitched battles with the Demonists.'

'You mean the antigalactics?' Falkayn rubbed his chin. The bristles made a scratchy noise, in the ceaseless gentle thrum that filled the cabin. He inhaled the sour smell of his own weariness. 'Maybe they did this.'

'I doubt that. They must be investigated, naturally – a major undertaking in itself – but they do not appear sufficiently well organized.'

'Damnation, if we don't get her back I'm going to push for letting this whole race stew!'

'You will not succeed. And in any event, it would be unjust to let millions die for the crime of a few.'

'The millions jolly well ought to be tracking down the few. It's possible. There have to be some leads somewhere. If every single one is followed –'

The detector panel flickered. Muddlehead announced: 'Ship observed. A chemical carrier, I believe, from the outer system. Range –'

'Oh, dry up,' Falkayn said, 'and blow away.'

'I am not equipped to –'

Falkayn stabbed the voice cutoff button.

He sat for a while, then, staring into the stars. His pipe went out unnoticed between his fingers. Adzel sighed and laid his head down on the deck.

'Poor little Chee,' Falkayn whispered at last. 'She came a long way to die.'

'Most likely she lives,' Adzel said.

'I hope so. But she used to go flying through trees, in an endless forest. Being caged will kill her.'

'Or unbalance her mind. She is so easily infuriated. If anger can find no object, it turns to feed on itself.'

'Well . . . you were always squabbling with her.'

'It meant nothing. Afterward she would cook me a special dinner. Once I admired a painting of hers, and she thrust it into my hands and said, "Take the silly thing, then," like a cub that is too shy to say it loves you.'

'Uh-huh.'

The cutoff button popped up. 'Course adjustment required,' Muddlehead stated, 'in order to avoid dangerously close passage by ore carrier.'

'Well, do it,' Falkayn rasped, 'and I wish those bastards joy of their ores. Destruction, but they've got a lot of space traffic!'

'Well, we are in the ecliptic plane, and as yet near Ronruad,' Adzel said. 'The coincidence is not great.'

Falkayn clenched his hands. The pipestem snapped. 'Suppose we strafe the ground,' he said in a cold strange voice. 'Not kill anyone. Burn up a few expensive installations, though, and promise more of the same if they don't get off their duffs and start a real search for her.'

'No. We have considerable discretion, but not that much.'

'We could argue with the board of inquiry later.'

'Such a deed would produce confusion and antagonism, and weaken the basis of the rescue effort. It might actually make rescue impossible. You have observed how basic pride is to the dominant Merseian cultures. An attempt to browbeat them, with no face-saving formula possible, might compel them to refuse galactic assistance. We would be personally, criminally responsible. I cannot permit it, David.'

'So we can't do anything, not anything, to – '

Falkayn's words chopped off. He smashed a fist down on the arm of his pilot chair and surged to his feet. Adzel rose also, sinews drawn taut. He knew his partner.

Merseia hung immense, shining with oceans, blazoned

86

with clouds and continents, rimmed with dawn and sunset and the deep sapphire of her sky. Her four small moons made a diadem. Korych flamed in plumage of zodiacal light.

Space cruiser *Yonuar*, United Fleet of the Great Vachs, swung close in polar orbit. Officially she was on patrol to stand by for possible aid to distressed civilian vessels. In fact she was there to keep an eye on the warcraft of Lafdigu, Wolder, the Nersan Alliance, any whom her masters mistrusted. And, yes, on the new-come galactics, if they returned hither. The God alone knew what they intended. One must tread warily and keep weapons close to hand.

On his command bridge, Captain Tryntaf Fangryf-Tamer gazed into the simulacrum tank and tried to imagine what laired among those myriad suns. He had grown up knowing that others flitted freely between them while his people were bound to this one system, and hating that knowledge. Now they were here once again . . . why? Too many rumors flew about. But most of them centered on the ominous spark called Valenderay. Help; collaboration; were the Vach Isthyr to become mere clients of some outworld grotesque?

A signal fluted. The intercom said: 'Radar Central to captain. Object detected on an intercept path.' The figures which followed were unbelievable. No meteoroid, surely, despite an absence of jet radiation. Therefore, the galactics! His black uniform tunic grew taut around Tryntaf's shoulders as he hunched forward and issued orders. Battle stations: not that he was looking for trouble, but he was prudent. And if trouble came, he'd much like to see how well the alien could withstand laser blasts and nuclear rockets.

She grew in his screens, a stubby truncated raindrop, ridiculously tiny against the sea-beast hulk of *Yonuar*.

She matched orbit so fast that Tryntaf heard the air suck in through his lips. Doom and death, why wasn't that hull broken apart and the crew smeared into a red layer? Some kind of counterfield . . . The vessel hung a few kilometers off and Tryntaf sought to calm himself. They would no doubt call him, and he must remain steady of nerve, cold of brain.

For his sealed orders mentioned that the galactics had left Merseia in anger, because the whole planet would not devote itself to a certain task. The Hands had striven for moderation; of course they would do what they reasonably could to oblige their guests from the stars, but they had other concerns too. The galactics seemed unable to agree that the business of entire worlds was more important than their private wishes. Of necessity, such an attitude was met with haughtiness, lest the name of the Vachs, of all the nations, be lowered.

Thus, when his outercom screen gave him an image, Tryntaf kept one finger on the combat button. He had some difficulty hiding his revulsion. Those thin features, shock of hair, tailless body, fuzzed brown skin, were like a dirty caricature of Merseiankind. He would rather have spoken to the companion, whom he could see in the background. That creature was honestly weird.

Nonetheless, Tryntaf got through the usual courtesies and asked the galactic's business in a level tone.

Falkayn had pretty well mastered modern language by now. 'Captain,' he said, 'I regret this and apologize, but you'll have to return to base.'

Tryntaf's heart slammed. Only his harness prevented him from jerking backward, to drift across the bridge in the dreamlike flight of zero gravity. He swallowed and managed to keep his speech calm. 'What is the reason?'

'We have communicated it to different leaders,' said

Falkayn, 'but since they don't accept the idea, I'll also explain to you personally.

'Someone, we don't know who, has kidnapped a crew member of ours. I'm sure that you, Captain, will understand that honor requires we get her back.'

'I do,' Tryntaf said, 'and honor demands that we assist you. But what has this to do with my ship?'

'Let me go on, please. I want to prove that no offense is intended. We have little time to make ready for the coming disaster, and few personnel to employ. The contribution of each is vital. In particular, the specialized knowledge of our vanished teammate cannot be dispensed with. So her return is of the utmost importance to all Merseians.'

Tryntaf grunted. He knew the argument was specious, meant to provide nothing but an acceptable way for his people to capitulate to the strangers' will.

'The search for her looks hopeless when she can be moved about in space,' Falkayn said. 'Accordingly, while she is missing, interplanetary traffic must be halted.'

Tryntaf rapped an oath. 'Impossible.'

'Contrariwise,' Falkayn said. 'We hope for your cooperation, but if your duty forbids this, we too can enforce the decree.'

Tryntaf was astonished to hear himself, through a tide of fury, say just: 'I have no such orders.'

'That is regrettable,' Falkayn said. 'I know your superiors will issue them, but that takes time and the emergency will not wait. Be so good as to return to base.'

Tryntaf's finger poised over the button. 'And if I don't?'

'Captain, we shouldn't risk damage to your fine ship – '

Tryntaf gave the signal.

His gunners had the range. Beams and rockets vomited forth.

Not one missile hit. The enemy flitted aside, letting them pass, as if they were thrown pebbles. A full-power ray struck: but not her hull. Energy sparked and showered blindingly off some invisible barrier.

The little vessel curved about like an aircraft. One beam licked briefly from her snout. Alarms resounded. Damage Control cried, near hysteria, that armorplate had been sliced off as a knife might cut soft wood. No great harm done; but if the shot had been directed at the reaction-mass tanks –

'How very distressing, Captain,' Falkayn said. 'But accidents will happen when weapons systems are overly automated, don't you agree? For the sake of your crew, for the sake of your country whose ship is your responsibility, I do urge you to reconsider.'

'Hold fire,' Tryntaf gasped.

'You will return planetside, then?' Falkayn asked.

'I curse you, yes,' Tryntaf said with a parched mouth.

'Good. You are a wise male, Captain. I salute you. Ah . . . you may wish to notify your fellow commanders elsewhere, so they can take steps to assure there will be no further accidents. Meanwhile, though, please commence re-entry.'

Jets stabbed into space. *Yonuar*, pride of the Vachs, began her inward spiral.

And aboard *Muddlin' Through*, Falkayn wiped his brow and grinned shakily at Adzel. 'For a minute,' he said, 'I was afraid that moron was going to slug it out.'

'We could have disabled his command with no casualties,' Adzel said, 'and I believe they have lifecraft.'

'Yes, but think of the waste; and the grudge.' Falkayn shook himself. 'Come on, let's get started. We've a lot of others to round up.'

'Can we – a lone civilian craft – blockade an entire

globe?' Adzel wondered. 'I do not recall that it has ever been done.'

'No, I don't imagine it has. But that's because the opposition has also had things like grav drive. These Merseian rowboats are something else again. And we need only watch this one planet. Everything funnels through it.' Falkayn stuffed tobacco into a pipe. 'Uh, Adzel, suppose you compose our broadcast to the public. You're more tactful than I am.'

'What shall I say?' the Wodenite asked.

'Oh, the same guff as I just forked out, but dressed up and tied with a pink ribbon.'

'Do you really expect this to work, David?'

'I've pretty high hopes. Look, all we'll call for is that Chee be left some safe place and we be notified where. We'll disavow every intention of punishing anybody, and we can make that plausible by pointing out that the galactics have to prove they're as good as their word if their mission is to have any chance of succeeding. If the kidnappers don't oblige – Well, first, they'll have the entire population out on a full-time hunt after them. And second, they themselves will be suffering badly from the blockade meanwhile. Whoever they are. Because you wouldn't have as much interplanetary shipping as you do, if it weren't basic to the economy.'

Adzel shifted in unease. 'We must not cause anyone to starve.'

'We won't. Food isn't sent across space, except gourmet items; too costly. How often do I have to explain to you, old thickhead? What we will cause is that everybody loses money. Megacredits per diem. And Very Important Merseians will be stranded in places like Luridor, and they'll burn up the maser beams ordering their subordinates to remedy that state of affairs. And factories will shut down, spaceports lie idle, investments crumble, political and military balances get upset . . . You can fill in the details.'

Falkayn lit his pipe and puffed a blue cloud. 'I don't expect matters will go that far, actually,' he went on. 'The Merseians are as able as us to foresee the consequences. Not a hypothetical disaster three years hence, but money and power eroding away right now. So they'll put it first on their agenda to find those kidnappers and take out resentment on them. The kidnappers will know this and will also, I trust, be hit in their personal breadbasket. I bet in a few days they'll offer to swap Chee for an amnesty.'

'Which I trust we will honor,' Adzel said.

'I told you we'll have to. Wish we didn't.'

'Please don't be so cynical, David. I hate to see you lose merit.'

Falkayn chuckled. 'But I make profits. Come on, Muddlehead, get busy and find us another ship.'

The teleconference room in Castle Afon could handle a sealed circuit that embraced the world. On this day it did.

Falkayn sat in a chair he had brought, looking across a table scarred by the daggers of ancestral warriors, to the mosaic of screens which filled the opposite wall. A hundred or more Merseian visages lowered back at him. On that scale, they had no individuality. Save one: a black countenance ringed by empty frames. No lord would let his image stand next to that of Haguan Eluatz.

Beside the human, Morruchan, Hand of the Vach Dathyr, rose and said with frigid ceremoniousness: 'In the name of the God and the blood, we are met. May we be well met. May wisdom and honor stand shield to shield – ' Falkayn listened with half an ear. He was busy rehearsing his speech. At best, he was in for a cobalt bomb's worth of trouble.

No danger, of course. *Muddlin' Through* hung plain in sight above Ardaig. Television carried that picture around Merseia. And it linked him to Adzel and Chee Lan, who waited at the guns. He was protected.

But what he had to say could provoke a wrath so great that his mission was wrecked. He must say it with infinite care, and then he must hope.

' – obligation to a guest demands we hear him out,' Morruchan finished brusquely.

Falkayn stood up. He knew that in those eyes he was a monster, whose motivations were not understandable and who had proven himself dangerous. So he had dressed in his plainest gray zipsuit, and was unarmed, and spoke in soft words.

'Worthies,' he said, 'forgive me that I do not use your title, for you are of many ranks and nations. But you are those who decide for your whole race. I hope you will feel free to talk as frankly as I shall. This is a secret and informal conference, intended to explore what is best for Merseia.

'Let me first express my heartfelt gratitude for your selfless and successful labors to get my teammate returned unharmed. And let me also thank you for indulging my wish that the, uh, chieftain Haguan Eluatz participate in this honorable assembly, albeit he has no right under law to do so. The reason shall soon be explained. Let me, finally, once again express my regret at the necessity of stopping your space commerce, for however brief a period, and my thanks for your cooperation in this emergency measure. I hope that you will consider any losses made good, when my people arrive to help you rescue your civilization.

'Now, then, it is time we put away whatever is past and look to the future. Our duty is to organize that great task. And the problem is, how shall it be organized? The galactic technologists do not wish to usurp any Merseian authority. In fact, they could not. They will be too few, too foreign, and too busy. If they are to do their work in the short time available, they must accept the guidance of the powers that be. They must make heavy use of existing facilities. That, of course, must be authorized by those who control the facilities. I need not elaborate. Experienced leaders like yourselves, worthies, can easily grasp what is entailed.'

He cleared his throat. 'A major question, obviously, is: with whom shall our people work most closely? They have no desire to discriminate. Everyone will be consulted, within the sphere of his time-honored prerogatives. Everyone will be aided, as far as possible. Yet, plain to see, a committee of the whole would be impossibly large and diverse. For setting overall policy, our people require a small, unified Merseian council, whom they can get to know really well and with whom they can develop effective decision-making procedures.

'Furthermore, the resources of this entire system must be used in a coordinated way. For example, Country One cannot be allowed to hoard minerals which Country Two needs. Shipping must be free to go from any point to any other. And all available shipping must be pressed into service. We can furnish radiation screens for your vessels, but we cannot furnish the vessels themselves in the numbers that are needed. Yet at the same time, a certain amount of ordinary activity must continue. People will still have to eat, for instance. So – how do we make a fair allocation of resources and establish a fair system of priorities?

'I think these considerations make it obvious to you, worthies, that an international organization is absolutely essential, one which can *impartially* supply information, advice, and coordination. If it has facilities and workers of its own, so much the better.

'Would that such an organization had legal existence! But it does not, and I doubt there is time to form one. If you will pardon me for saying so, worthies, Merseia is burdened with too many old hatreds and jealousies to join overnight in brotherhood. In fact, the international group must be watched carefully, lest it try to aggrandize itself or diminish others. We galactics can do this with one organization. We cannot with a hundred.

'So.' Falkayn longed for his pipe. Sweat prickled his skin. 'I have no plenipotentiary writ. My team is merely supposed to make recommendations. But the matter is so urgent that whatever scheme we propose will likely be adopted, for the sake of getting on with the job. And we have found one group which transcends the rest. It pays no attention to barriers between people and people. It is large, powerful, rich, disciplined, efficient. It is not exactly what my civilization would prefer as its chief instrument for the deliverance of Merseia. We would honestly rather it went down the drain, instead of becoming yet more firmly entrenched. But we have a saying that necessity knows no law.'

He could feel the tension gather, like a thunderstorm boiling up; he heard the first rageful retorts; he said fast, before the explosion came: 'I refer to the Gethfennu.'

What followed was indescribable.

But he was, after all, only warning of what his report would be. He could point out that he bore a grudge of his own, and was setting it aside for the common good. He could even, with considerable enjoyment, throw some imaginative remarks about ancestry and habits in the direction of Haguan – who grinned and looked smug. In the end, hours later, the assembly agreed to take the proposal under advisement. Falkayn knew what the upshot would be. Merseia had no choice.

The screens blanked.

Wet, shaking, exhausted, he looked across a stillness into the face of Morruchan Long-Ax. The Hand loomed over him. Fingers twitched longingly near a pistol butt. Morruchan said, biting off each word: 'I trust you realize what you are doing. You're not just perpetuating that gang. You're conferring legitimacy on them. They will be able to claim they are now a part of recognized society.'

'Won't they, then, have to conform to its laws?' Falkayn's larynx hurt, his voice was husky.

'Not them!' Morruchan stood brooding a moment. 'But a reckoning will come. The Vachs will prepare one, if nobody else does. And afterward – Are you going to teach us how to build stargoing ships?'

'Not if I have any say in the matter,' Falkayn replied.

'Another score. Not important in the long run. We're bound to learn a great deal else, and on that basis . . . well, galactic, our grandchildren will see.'

'Is ordinary gratitude beneath your dignity?'

'No. There'll be enough soft-souled dreambuilders, also among my race, for an orgy of sentimentalism. But then you'll go home again. I will abide.'

Falkayn was too tired to argue. He made his formal farewells and called the ship to come get him.

Later, hurtling through the interstellar night, he listened to Chee's tirade: ' – I still have to get back at those grease-paws. They'll be sorry they ever touched me.'

'You don't aim to return, do you?' Falkayn asked.

'Pox, no!' she said. 'But the engineers on Merseia will need recreation. The Gethfennu will supply some of it, gambling especially, I imagine. Now if I suggest our lads carry certain miniaturized gadgets which can, for instance, control a wheel –'

Adzel sighed. 'In this splendid and terrible cosmos,' he said, 'why must we living creatures be forever perverse?'

A smile tugged at Falkayn's mouth. 'We wouldn't have so much fun otherwise,' he said.

Men and not-men were still at work when the supernova wavefront reached Merseia.

Suddenly the star filled the southern night, a third as brilliant as Korych, too savage for the naked eye to look at. Blue-white radiance flooded the land, shadows were etched sharp, trees and hills stood as if illuminated by lightning. Wings beat upward from forests, animals cried through the troubled air, drums pulsed and prayers lifted in villages which once had feared the dark for which they now longed. The day that followed was lurid and furious.

Over the months, the star faded, until it became a knife-keen point and scarcely visible when the sun was aloft. But it waxed in beauty, for its radiance excited the gas around it, so that it gleamed amidst a whiteness which deepened at the edge to blue-violet and a nebular lace-work which shone with a hundred faerie hues. Thence also, in Merseia's heaven, streamed huge shuddering banners of aurora, whose whisper was heard even on the ground. An odor of storm was blown on every wind.

Then the nuclear rain began. And nothing was funny any longer.

Also in the records left on Hermes was information about an episode which had long been concealed: how Nicholas van Rijn came to the world which today we know as Mirkheim. The reasons for secrecy at the time are self-evident. Later they did not obtain. However, it is well known that Falkayn was always reluctant to mention his part in the origins of the Supermetals enterprise, and curt-spoken whenever the subject was forced upon him. Given all else there was to strive with in the beginning upon Avalon, it is no flaw of wind that folk did not press their leaders about this, and that the matter dropped from general awareness. Even before then, he had done what he could to suppress details.

Of course, the alatan facts are in every biography of the Founder. Yet this one affair is new to us. It helps explain much which followed, especially his reserve, rare in an otherwise cheerful and outgoing person. In truth, it gives us a firmer grip than we had before upon the reality of him.

The records contain only the ship's log for that voyage,

plus some taped conversations, data lists, and the like. However, these make meaningful certain hitherto cryptic references in surviving letters written by Coya to her husband. Furthermore, with the identity of vessel and captain known, it became possible to enlist the aid of the Wryfields Choth on Ythri. Stirrok, its Wyvan, was most helpful in finding Hirharouk's private journal, while his descendants kindly agreed to waive strict rightness and allow it to be read.

From these sources, Hloch and Arinnian have composed the narrative which follows.

Lightning reached. David Falkayn heard the crack of torn air and gulped a rainy reek of ozone. His cheek stung from the near miss. In his eyes, spots of blue-white dazzle danced across night.

'Get aboard, you two,' Adzel said. 'I'll hold them.'

Crouched, Falkayn peered after a target for his own blaster. He saw shadows move beneath strange constellations – that, and flames which tinged upward-rolling smoke on the far side of the spacefield, where the League outpost was burning. Shrieks resounded. 'No, you start,' he rasped. 'I'm armed, you're not.'

The Wodenite's bass remained steady, but an earthquake rumble entered it. 'No more deaths. A single death would have been too much, of folk outraged in their own homes. David, Chee: *go*.'

Half-dragon, half-centaur, four and a half meters from snout to tailtip, he moved toward the unseen natives. Firelight framed the hedge of bony plates along his back, glimmered off scales and bellyscutes.

Chee Lan tugged at Falkayn's trousers. 'Come on,' she

spat. 'No stopping that hairy-brain when he wambles off on an idealism binge. He won't board before us, and they'll kill him if we don't move fast.' A sneer: 'I'll lead the way, if that'll make you feel more heroic.'

Her small, white-furred form shot from the hauler behind which they had taken refuge. (No use trying to get that machine aloft. The primitives had planned their attack shrewdly, must have hoarded stolen explosives as well as guns for years, till they could demolish everything around the base at the same moment as they fell upon the headquarters complex.) Its mask-markings obscured her blunt-muzzled face in the shuddering red light; but her bottled-up tail stood all too clear.

A Tamethan saw. On long thin legs, beak agape in a war-yell, he sped to catch her. His weapon was merely a spear. Sick-hearted, Falkayn took aim. Then Chee darted between those legs, tumbled the autochthon on his tocus and bounded onward.

Hurry! Falkayn told himself. Battle ramped around Adzel. The Wodenite could take a certain number of slugs and blaster bolts without permanent damage, he knew, but not many . . . and those mighty arms were pulling their punches. Keeping to shadow as well as might be, the human followed Chee Lan.

Their ship loomed ahead, invulnerable to the attackers. Her gangway was descending. So the Cynthian had entered audio range, had called an order to the main computer . . . *Why didn't we tell Muddlehead to use initiative in case of trouble?* groaned Falkayn's mind. *Why didn't we at least carry radios to call for its help? Are we due for retirement? A sloppy trade pioneer is a dead trade pioneer.*

A turret gun flashed and boomed. Chee must have ordered that. It was a warning shot, sent skyward, but terrifying. The man gusted relief. His rangy body sped upramp, stopped at the open airlock, and turned to peer back. Combat seemed to have frozen. And, yes, here Adzel came, limping, trailing blood, but alive. Falkayn wanted to hug his old friend and weep.

No. First we haul mass out of here. He entered the ship. Adzel's hoofs boomed on the gangway. It retracted, the airlock closed, gravity drive purred, and *Muddlin' Through* ascended to heaven.

– Gathered on the bridge, her crew stared at a downward-viewing screen. The fires had become sparks, the spacefield a scar, in an illimitable night. Far off, a river cut through jungle, shining by starlight like a drawn sword.

Falkayn ran fingers through his sandy hair. 'We uh, well, do you think we can rescue any survivors?' he asked.

'I doubt there are any by now,' Adzel said. 'We barely escaped: because we have learned, over years, to meet emergencies as a team.'

'And if there are,' Chee added, 'who cares?' Adzel looked reproof at her. She bristled her whiskers. 'We saw how those slimesouls were treating the aborigines.'

'I feel sure much of the offense was caused simply by ignorance of basic psychology and mores.'

'That's no excuse, as you flapping well know. They should've taken the trouble to learn such things. But no, the companies couldn't wait for that. They sent their bespattered factors and field agents right in, who promptly set up a little dunghill of an empire – *Ya-pu-yeh!*' In Chee's home language that was a shocking obscenity, even for her.

Falkayn's shoulders slumped. 'I'm inclined to agree,' he said. 'Besides, we mustn't take risks. We've got to make a report.'

'Why?' Adzel asked. 'Our own employer was not involved.'

'No, thanks be. I'd hate to feel I must quit . . . This is League business, however. The mutual-assistance rule – '

'And so League warcraft come and bomb some poor little villages?' Adzel's tail drummed on the deck.

'With our testimony, we can hope not. The Council verdict ought to be, those klongs fell flat on their own deeds.' Falkayn sighed. 'I wish we'd been around here longer, making a regular investigation, instead of just chancing by and deciding to take a few days off on a pleasant planet.' He straightened. 'Well. To space, Muddlehead, and to – m-m-m, nearest major League base – Irumclaw.'

'And you come along to sickbay and let me dress those wounds, you overgrown bulligator,' Chee snapped at the Wodenite, 'before you've utterly ruined this carpet, drooling blood on it.'

Falkayn himself sought a washroom, a change of clothes, his pipe and tobacco, a stiff drink. Continuing to the saloon, he settled down and tried to ease away his trouble. In a viewscreen, the world dwindled which men had named Tametha – arbitrarily, from a native word in a single locality, which they'd doubtless gotten wrong anyway. Already it had shrunk in his vision to a ball, swirled blue and white: a body as big and fair as ever Earth was, four or five billion years in the making, uncounted swarms of unknown life forms, sentiences and civilizations, histories and mysteries, become a marble in a game . . . or a set of entries in a set of data banks, for profit or loss, in a few cities a hundred or more light-years remote.

He thought: *This isn't the first time I've seen undying wrong done. Is it really happening oftener and oftener, or am I just getting more aware of it as I age? At thirty-three, I begin to feel old.*

Chee entered, jumped onto the seat beside him, and reported Adzel was resting. 'You do need that drink, don't you?' she observed. Falkayn made no reply. She inserted a mildly narcotic cigarette in an interminable ivory holder and puffed it to ignition.

'Yes,' she said, 'I get irritated likewise, no end, whenever something like this befouls creation.'

'I'm coming to think the matter is worse, more fundamental, than a collection of episodes.' Falkayn spoke wearily. 'The Polesotechnic League began as a mutual-benefit association of companies, true; but the idea was also to keep competition within decent bounds. That's breaking down, that second aspect. How long till the first does too?'

'What would you prefer to free enterprise? The Terran Empire, maybe?'

'Well, you being a pure carnivore, and coming beside from a trading culture that was quick to modernize – exploitation doesn't touch you straight on the nerves, Chee. But Adzel – he doesn't say much, you know him, but I've become certain it's a bitterness to him, more and more as time slides by, that nobody will help his people advance . . . because they haven't anything that anybody wants enough to pay the price of advancement. And – well, I hardly dare guess how many others. Entire worlds-ful of beings who look at yonder stars till it aches in them, and know that except for a few lucky individuals, none of them will ever get out there, nor will their descendants have any real say about the future, no, will instead remain nothing but potential victims –'

Seeking distraction, Falkayn raised screen magnification and swept the scanner around jewel-blazing blackness. When he stopped for another pull at his glass, the view happened to include the enigmatic glow of the Crab Nebula.

'Take that sentimentalism and stuff it back where it came from,' Chee suggested. 'The new-discovered species will simply have to accumulate capital. Yours did. Mine did soon after. We can't give a free ride to the whole universe.'

'N-no. Yet you know yourself – be honest – how quick somebody already established would be to take away that bit of capital, whether by market manipulations or by thinly disguised piracy. Tametha's a minor example. All that those tribesbeings wanted was to trade directly with Over-the-Mountains.' Falkayn's fist clamped hard around his pipe. 'I tell you, lass, the heart is going out of the League, in the sense of ordinary compassion and helpfulness. How long till the heart goes out in the sense of its own survivability? Civilization *needs* more than the few monopolists we've got.'

The Cynthian twitched her ears, quite slowly, and exhaled smoke whose sweetness blent with the acridity of the man's tobacco. Her eyes glowed through it, emerald-hard. 'I sort of agree. At least, I'd enjoy listening to the hot air hiss out of certain bellies. How, though, Davy? How?'

'Old Nick – he's a single member of the Council, I realize –'

'Our dear employer keeps his hirelings fairly moral, but strictly on the principle of running a taut ship. He told me that himself once, and added, "Never mind what the ship is taught, ho, ho, ho!" No, you won't make an idealist of Nicholas van Rijn. Not without transmuting every atom in his fat body.'

Falkayn let out a tired chuckle. 'A new isotope. Van Rijn-235, no, likelier Vr-235,000 –'

And then his glance passed over the Nebula, and as if it had spoken to him across more than a thousand parsecs, he fell silent and grew tense where he sat.

This happened shortly after the Satan episode, when the owner of Solar Spice & Liquors had found it needful once more to leave the comforts of the Commonwealth, risk his thick neck on a cheerless world, and finally make a month-long voyage in a ship which had run out of beer. Returned home, he swore by all that was holy and much that was not: Never again!

Nor, for most of the following decade, had he any reason to break his vow. His business was burgeoning, thanks to excellently chosen personnel in established trade sites and to pioneers like the *Muddlin' Through* team who kept finding him profitable new lands. Besides, he had maneuvered himself into the overlordship of Satan. A sunless wandering planet, newly thawed out by a brush with a giant star, made a near-ideal site for the manufacture of odd isotopes on a scale commensurate with present-day demand. Such industry wasn't his cup of tea 'or', he declared, 'my glass Genever that molasses-on-Pluto-footed butler is supposed to bring me before I crumble away from thirst.' Therefore van Rijn granted franchises, on terms calculated to be an ångström short of impossibly extortionate.

Many persons wondered, often in colorful language, why he didn't retire and drink himself into a grave they would be glad to provide, outsize though it must be. When van Rijn heard about these remarks, he would grin and look still harder for a price he could jack up or a competitor he could undercut. Nevertheless, compared to earlier years, this was for him a leisured period. When at last word got around that he meant to take Coya Conyon, his favorite granddaughter, on an extended cruise aboard his yacht – and not a single mistress along for him – hope grew that he was slowing down to a halt.

I can't say I like most of those money-machine merchant princes, Coya reflected, several weeks after leaving

107

Earth; *but I really wouldn't want to give them heart attacks by telling them we're now on a nonhuman vessel, equipped in curious ways but unmistakably battle-ready, bound into a region that nobody is known to have explored.*

She stood before a viewport set in a corridor. A ship built by men would not have carried that extravagance; but to Ythrians, sky dwellers, ample outlook is a necessity of sanity. The air she breathed was a little thinner than at Terrestrial sea level; odors included the slight smokiness of their bodies. A ventilator murmured not only with draft but with a barely heard rustle, the distance-muffled sound of wingbeats from crewfolk off duty cavorting in an enormous hold intended for it. At 0.75 standard weight she still – after this long a trip – felt exhilaratingly light.

She was not presently conscious of that. At first she had reveled in adventure. Everything was an excitement; every day offered a million discoveries to be made. She didn't mind being the sole human aboard besides her grandfather. He was fun in his bearish fashion: had been as far back as she could remember, when he would roll roaring into her parents' home, toss her to the ceiling, half-bury her under presents from a score of planets, tell her extravagant stories and take her out on a sailboat or to a live performance or, later on, around most of the Solar System . . . Anyhow, to make Ythrian friends, to discover a little of how their psyches worked and how one differed from another, to trade music, memories, and myths, watch their aerial dances and show them some ballet, that was an exploration in itself.

Today, however – They were apparently nearing the goal for which they had been running in a search helix, whatever it was. Van Rijn remained boisterous; but he would tell her nothing. Nor did the Ythrians know what was sought, except for Hirharouk, and he had passed on no other information than that all were to hold themselves prepared for emergencies cosmic or warlike. A species whose ancestors had lived like eagles could take this more easily than men. Even so, tension had mounted till she could smell it.

Her gaze sought outward. As an astrophysicist and a fairly frequent tourist, she had spent a total of years in space during the twenty-five she had been in the universe. She could identify the brightest individual stars amidst that radiant swarm, lacy and lethal loveliness of shining nebulae, argent torrent of Milky Way, remote glimmer of sister galaxies. And still size and silence, unknownness and unknowability, struck against her as much as when she first fared forth.

Secrets eternal . . . why, of course. They had run at a good pseudovelocity for close to a month, starting at Ythri's sun (which lies 278 light-years from Sol in the direction of Lupus) and aiming at the Deneb sector. That put them, oh, say a hundred parsecs from Earth. Glib calculation. Yet they had reached parts which no record said anyone had ever done more than pass through, in all the centuries since men got a hyperdrive. The planetary systems here had not been catalogued, let alone visited, let alone understood. Space is that big, that full of worlds.

Coya shivered, though the air was warm enough. *You're yonder somewhere, David,* she thought, *if you haven't met the inevitable final surprise. Have you gotten my message? Did it have any meaning to you?*

She could do nothing except give her letter to another trade pioneer whom she trusted. He was bound for the same general region as Falkayn had said *Muddlin' Through* would next go questing in. The crews maintained rendezvous stations. In one such turbulent place he might get news of Falkayn's team. Or he could deposit the letter there to be called for.

Guilt nagged her, as it had throughout this journey. A betrayal of her grandfather – No! Fresh anger flared. *If he's not brewing something bad, what possible harm can it do him that David knows what little I knew before we left – which is scarcely more than the old devil has let me know to this hour?*

And he did speak of hazards. I did have to force him into taking me along (because the matter seemed to concern you, David, oh, David). If we meet trouble, and suddenly you arrive –

Stop romancing, Coya told herself. *You're a grown girl now.* She found she could control her thoughts, somewhat, but not the tingle through her blood.

She stood tall, slender almost to boyishness, clad in plain black tunic, slacks, and sandals. Straight dark hair, shoulder-length, framed an oval face with a snub nose, mouth a trifle too wide but eyes remarkably big and gold-flecked green. Her skin was very white. It was rather freakish how genes had recombined to forget nearly every trace of her ancestry – van Rijn's Dutch and Malay; the Mexican and Chinese of a woman who bore him a girl-child and with whom he had remained on the same amicable terms afterwards as, somehow, he did with most former loves; the Scots (from Hermes, David's home planet) plus a dash of African (via a planet called Nyanza) in that Malcolm Conyon who settled down on Earth and married Beatriz Yeo.

Restless, Coya's mind skimmed over the fact. Her lips could not help quirking. *In short, I'm a typical modern human.* The amusement died. *Yes, also in my life. My grandfather's generation seldom bothered to get married. My father's did. And mine, why, we're reviving patrilineal surnames.*

A whistle snapped off her thinking. Her heart lurched until she identified the signal. 'All hands alert.'

That meant something had been detected. Maybe not the goal; maybe just a potential hazard, like a meteoroid swarm. In uncharted space, you traveled warily, and van Rijn kept a candle lit before his little Martian sandroot statuette of St Dismas.

A moment longer, Coya confronted the death and glory beyond the ship. Then, fists knotted, she strode aft. She was her grandfather's granddaughter.

'Lucifer and leprosy!' bellowed Nicholas van Rijn. 'You have maybe spotted what we maybe are after, at extreme range of your instruments tuned sensitive like an artist what specializes in painting pansies, a thing we cannot reach in enough hours to eat three good rijstaffels, and you have the bladder to tell me I got to armor me and stand around crisp saying, "Aye-yi-yi, sir?" ' Sprawled in a lounger, he waved a two-liter tankard of beer he clutched in his hairy left paw. The right held a churchwarden pipe, which had filled his stateroom with blue reek.

Hirharouk of the Wryfields Choth, captain of the chartered ranger *Gaiian* (= *Dewfall*), gave him look for look. The Ythrian's eyes were large and golden, the man's small and black and crowding his great hook nose; neither pair gave way, and Hirharouk's answer held an iron quietness: 'No. I propose that you stop guzzling alcohol. You do have drugs to induce sobriety, but they may show side effects when quick decision is needed.'

While his Anglic was fluent, he used a vocalizer to convert the sounds he could make into clearly human tones. The Ythrian voice is beautifully ringing but less flexible than man's. Was it to gibe or be friendly that van Rijn responded in pretty fair Planha? 'Be not perturbed. I am hardened, which is why my vices cost me a fortune.

111

Moreover, a body my size has corresponding capacity.' He slapped the paunch beneath his snuff-stained blouse and gaudy sarong. The rest of him was huge in proportion. 'This is my way of resting in advance of trouble, even as you would soar aloft and contemplate.'

Hirharouk eased and fluted his equivalent of a laugh. 'As you wish. I daresay you would not have survived to this date, all the sworn foes you must have, did you not know what you do.'

Van Rijn tossed back his sloping brow. Long swarthy ringlets in the style of his youth, except for their greasiness, swirled around the jewels in his earlobes; his chins quivered beneath waxed mustaches and goatee; a bare splay foot smote the densely carpeted deck. 'You mistake me,' he boomed, reverting to his private version of Anglic. 'You cut me to the quiche. Do you suppose I, poor old lonely sinner, *ja*, but still a Christian man with a soul full of hope, do you suppose *I* ever went after anything but peace – as many peaces as I could get? No, no, what I did, I was pushed into, self-defense against sons of mothers, greedy rascals who I may forgive though God cannot, who begrudge me what tiny profit I need so I not become a charge on a state that is only good for grinding up taxpayers anyway. Me, I am like gentle St Francis, I go around ripping off olive branches and covering stormy seas with oil slicks and watering troubled fish.'

He stuck his tankard under a spout at his elbow for a refill. Hirharouk observed him. And Coya, entering the disordered luxury of the stateroom, paused to regard them both.

She was fond of van Rijn. Her doubts about this expedition, the message she had felt she must try to send to David Falkayn, had been a sharp blade in her. Nonetheless she admitted the Ythrian was infinitely more sightly. Handsomer than her too, she felt, or David himself. That was especially true in flight; yet, slow and awkward though they were aground, the Ythrians remained magnificent to see, and not only because of the born hunter's inborn pride.

Hirharouk stood some 150 centimeters tall. What he stood on was his wings, which spanned five and a half meters when unfolded. Turned downward, they spread claws at the angle which made a kind of foot; the backward-sweeping alatan surface could be used for extra support. What had been legs and talons, geological epochs ago, were arms and three-finger two-thumbed hands. The skin on those was amber-colored. The rest of him wore shimmering bronze feathers, save where these became black-edged white on crest and on fan-shaped tail. His body looked avian, stiff behind its jutting keelbone. But he was no bird. He had not been hatched. His head, raised on a powerful neck, had no beak: rather, a streamlined muzzle, nostrils at the tip, below them a mouth whose lips seemed oddly delicate against the keen fangs.

And the splendor of these people goes beyond the sunlight on them when they ride the wind, Coya thought. *David frets about the races that aren't getting a chance. Well, Ythri was primitive when the Grand Survey found it. The Ythrians studied Technic civilization, and neither licked its boots nor let it overwhelm them, but took what they wanted from it and made themselves a power in our corner of the galaxy. True, this was before that civilization was itself overwhelmed by* laissez-faire *capitalism* –

She blinked. Unlike her, the merchant kept his quarters at Earth-standard illumination; and Quetlan is yellower than Sol. He was used to abrupt transitions. She coughed in the tobacco haze. The two males grew aware of her.

'Ah, my sweet bellybird,' van Rijn greeted, a habit he had not shaken from the days of her babyhood. 'Come in. Flop yourself.' A gesture of his pipe gave a choice of an extra lounger, a desk chair, an emperor-size bed, a sofa between the liquor cabinet and the bookshelf, or the deck. 'What you want? Beer, gin, whisky, cognac, vodka, arrack, akvavit, half-dozen kinds of wine and liqueur, ansa, totipot, slumthunder, maryjane, ops, galt, Xanadu radium, or maybe – ' he winced ' – a soft drink? A soft, flabby drink?'

'Coffee will do, thanks.' Coya drew breath and courage. '*Gunung Tuan,* I've got to talk with you.'

'Ja, I outspected you would. Why I not told you more before is because – oh, I wanted you should enjoy your trip, not brood like a hummingbird on ostrich eggs.'

Coya was unsure whether Hirharouk spoke in tact or truth: 'Freeman van Rijn, I came to discuss our situation. Now I return to the bridge. For honor and life ... *khr-r-r,* I mean please ... hold ready for planlaying as information lengthens.' He lifted an arm. 'Freelady Conyon, hail and fare you well.'

He walked from them. When he entered the bare corridor, his claws clicked. He stopped and did a handstand. His wings spread as wide as possible in that space, preventing the door from closing till he was gone, exposing and opening the gill-like slits below them. He worked the wings, forcing those antlibranchs to operate like bellows. They were part of the 'supercharger' system which enabled a creature his size to fly under basically terrestroid conditions. Coya did not know whether he was oxygenating his bloodstream to energize himself for command, or was flushing out human stench.

He departed. She stood alone before her grandfather.

'Do sit, sprawl, hunker, or how you can best relax,' the man urged. 'I would soon have asked you should come. Time is to make a clean breast, except mine is too shaggy and you do not take off your tunic.' His sigh turned into a belch. 'A shame. Customs has changed. Not that I would lech in your case, no, I got incest repellent. But the sight is nice.'

She reddened and signalled the coffeemaker. Van Rijn clicked his tongue. 'And you don't smoke neither,' he said. 'Ah, they don't put the kind of stuff in youngsters like when I was your age.'

'A few of us try to exercise some forethought as well as our consciences,' Coya snapped. After a pause: 'I'm sorry. Didn't mean to sound self-righteous.'

'But you did. I wonder, has David Falkayn influenced you that way, or you him? – Ho-ho, a spectroscope would think your face was receding at speed of light!' Van Rijn wagged his pipestem. 'Be careful. He's a good boy, him, except he's not a boy no more. Could well be, without knowing it, he got somewhere a daughter old as you.'

'We're friends,' Coya said half-furiously. She sat down on the edge of the spare lounger, ignored its attempts to match her contours, twined fingers between knees, and glared into his twinkle. 'What the chaos do you expect my state of mind to be, when you wouldn't tell me what we're heading for?'

'You did not have to come along. You shoved in on me, armored in black mail.'

Coya did not deny the amiably made statement. She had threatened to reveal the knowledge she had gained at his request, and thereby give his rivals the same clues. He hadn't been too hard to persuade; after warning her of possible danger, he growled that he would be needing an astrophysicist and might as well keep things in the family.

I hope, God, how I hope he believes my motive was a hankering for adventure as I told him! He ought to believe it, and flatter himself I've inherited a lot of his instincts . . . No, he can't have guessed my real reason was

115

the fear that David is involved, in a wrong way. If he knew that, he need only have told me, 'Blab and be damned,' and I'd have had to stay home, silent. As is . . . David, in me you have here an advocate, whatever you may have done.

'I could understand your keeping me ignorant while we were on the yacht,' she counterattacked. 'No matter how carefully picked the crew, one of them might have been a commercial or government spy and might have managed to eavesdrop. But when, when in the Quetlan System we transferred to this vessel, and the yacht proceeded as if we were still aboard, and won't make any port for weeks – why didn't you speak?'

'Maybe I wanted you should for punishment be like a Yiddish brothel.'

'What?'

'Jews in your own stew. Haw, haw, haw!' She didn't smile. Van Rijn continued: 'Mainly, here again I could not be full-up sure of the crew. Ythrians is fearless and I suppose more honest by nature than men. But that is saying microbial little, *nie?* Here too we might have been overheard and – Well, Hirharouk agreed, he could not either absolute predict how certain of them would react. He tried but was not able to recruit everybody from his own choth.' The Planha word designated a basic social unit, more than a tribe, less than a nation, with cultural and religious dimensions corresponding to nothing human. 'Some, even, is from different societies and belong to no choths at allses. Ythrians got as much variation as the Commonwealth – no, more, because they not had time yet for technology to make them into homogeneouses.'

The coffeemaker chimed. Coya rose, tapped a cup, sat back down, and sipped. The warmth and fragrance were a point of comfort in an infinite space.

'We had a long trek ahead of us,' the merchant proceeded, 'and a lot of casting about, before we found what it *might* be we are looking for. Meanwhiles Hirharouk, and me as best I was able, sounded out those crewbeings not from Wryfields, got to understand them a weenie bit and – Hokay, he thinks we can trust them, regardless how the truth shapes up or ships out. And now, like you know, we have detected an object which could well be the simple, easy, small dissolution to the riddle.'

'What's small about a supernova?' Coya challenged. 'Even an extinct one?'

'When people ask me how I like being old as I am,' van Rijn said circuitously, 'I tell them, "Not bad when I consider the alternative." Bellybird, the alternative here would make the Shenn affair look like a game of peggletymum.'

Coya came near spilling her coffee. She had been adolescent when the sensation exploded: that the Polesotechnic League had been infiltrated by agents of a nonhuman species, dwelling beyond the regions which Technic civilization dominated and bitterly hostile to it; that war had barely been averted; that the principal rescuers were her grandfather and the crew of a ship named *Muddlin' Through*. On that day David Falkayn was unknowingly promoted to god (j.g.). She wondered if he knew it yet, or knew that their occasional outings together after she matured had added humanness without reducing that earlier rank.

Van Rijn squinted at her. 'You guessed we was hunting for a supernova remnant?' he probed.

She achieved a dry tone: 'Since you had me investigate the problem, and soon thereafter announced your plans for a "vacation trip", the inference was fairly obvious.'

'Any notion why I should want a white dwarf or a black hole instead of a nice glass red wine?'

Her pulse knocked. 'Yes, I think I've reasoned it out.'

And I think David may have done so before either of us, almost ten years ago. When you, Grandfather, asked me to use in secret –

– the data banks and computers at Luna Astrocenter, where she worked, he had given a typically cryptic reason. 'Could be this leads to a nice gob of profit nobody else's nose should root around in because mine is plenty big enough.' She didn't blame him for being close-mouthed, then. The League's self-regulation was breaking down, competition grew ever more literally cutthroat, and governments snarled not only at the capitalists but at each other. The Pax Mercatoria was drawing to an end and, while she had never wholly approved of it, she sometimes dreaded the future.

The task he set her was sufficiently interesting to blot out her fears. However unimaginably violent, the suicides of giant suns by supernova bursts, which may outshine a hundred billion living stars, are not rare cosmic events. The remains, in varying stages of decay – white dwarfs, neutron stars, in certain cases those eldritch not-quite-things known as black holes – are estimated to number fifty million in our galaxy alone. But its arms spiral across a hundred thousand light-years. In this raw immensity, the prospects of finding by chance a body the size of a smallish planet or less, radiating corpse-feebly if at all, are negligible.

(The analogy with biological death and decomposition is not morbid. Those lay the foundation for new life and further evolution. Supernovae, hurling atoms together in fusing fury, casting them forth into space as their own final gasps, have given us all the heavier elements, some of them vital, in our worlds and our bodies.)

No one hitherto had – openly – attempted a more subtle search. The scientists had too much else to do, as discovery exploded outward. Persons who wished to study supernova processes saw a larger variety of known cases than could be dealt with in lifetimes. Epsilon Aurigae, Sirius B, and Valenderay were simply among the most famous examples.

Coya in Astrocenter had at her beck every fact which Technic civilization had ever gathered about the stellar part of the universe. From the known distribution of former supernovae, together with data on other star types, dust, gas, radiation, magnetism, present location and concentrations, the time derivatives of these quantities: using well-established theories of galactic development, it is possible to compute with reasonable probability the distribution of undiscovered dark giants within a radius of a few hundred parsecs.

The problem is far more complex than that, of course; and the best of self-programming computers still needs a highly skilled sophont riding close herd on it, if anything is to be accomplished. Nor will the answers be absolute, even within that comparatively tiny sphere to which their validity is limited. The most you can learn is the likelihood (not the certainty) of a given type of object existing within such-and-such a distance of yourself, and the likeliest (not the indubitable) direction. To phrase it more accurately, you get a hierarchy of decreasingly probable solutions.

This suffices. If you have the patience, and money, to search on a path defined by the equations, you *will* in time find the kind of body you are interested in.

Coya had taken for granted that no one before van Rijn had been that interested. But the completeness of Astrocenter's electronic records extended to noting who had run which program when. The purpose was to avoid duplication of effort, in an era when nobody could keep up with the literature in the smallest speciality. Out of habit rather than logic, Coya called for this information and –

– *I found out that ten years earlier, David wanted to know precisely what you, Grandfather, now did. But he never told you, nor said where he and his partners went afterward, or anything.* Pain: *Nor has he told me. And I have not told you. Instead, I made you take me along; and before leaving, I sent David a letter saying everything I knew and suspected.*

Resolution: *All right, Nick van Rijn! You keep complaining about how moralistic my generation is. Let's see how you like getting some cards off the bottom of the deck!*

Yet she could not hate an old man who loved her.

'What do you mean by your "alternative?"' she whispered.

'Why, simple.' He shrugged like a mountain sending off an avalanche. 'If we do not find a retired supernova, being used in a way as original as spinning the peach basket, then we are up against a civilization outside ours, infiltrating ours, same as the Shenna did – except this one got technology would make ours let go in its diapers and scream, "Papa, Papa, in the closet is a boogeyman!"' Unaccustomed grimness descended on him. 'I think, in that case, really is a boogeyman, too.'

Chill entered her guts. 'Supermetals?'

'What else?' He took a gulp of beer. 'Ha, you is guessed what got me started was Supermetals?'

She finished her coffee and set the cup on a table. It rattled loud through a stretching silence. 'Yes,' she said at length, flat-voiced. 'You've given me a lot of hours to puzzle over what this expedition is for.'

'A jigsaw puzzle it is indeed, girl, and us sitting with bottoms snuggled in front of the jigsaw.'

'In view of the very, very special kind of supernova-and-companion you thought might be somewhere not too

120

far from Sol, and wanted me to compute about – in view of that, and of what Supermetals is doing, sure, I've arrived at a guess.'

'Has you likewise taken into account the fact Supermetals is not just secretive about everything like is its right, but refuses to join the League?'

'That's also its right.'

'Truly true. Nonetheleast, the advantages of belonging is maybe not what they used to was; but they do outweigh what small surrender of anatomy is required.'

'You mean autonomy, don't you?'

'I suppose. Must be I was thinking of women. A stern chaste is a long chaste . . . But you never got impure thoughts.' Van Rijn had the tact not to look at her while he rambled, and to become serious again immediately: 'You better hope, you heathen, and I better pray, the supermetals what the agents of Supermetals is peddling do not come out of a furnace run by anybody except God Himself.'

The primordial element, with which creation presumably began, is hydrogen-1, a single proton accompanied by a single electron. To this day, it comprises the overwhelming bulk of matter in the universe. Vast masses of it condensed into globes, which grew hot enough from that infall to light thermonuclear fires. Atoms melted together, forming higher elements. Novae, supernovae – and, less picturesquely but more importantly, smaller suns shedding gas in their red giant phase – spread these through space, to enter into later generations of stars. Thus came planets, life, and awareness.

Throughout the periodic table, many isotopes are radioactive. From polonium (number 84) on, none are stable. Protons packed together in that quantity generate forces of repulsion with which the forces of attraction cannot forever cope. Sooner or later, these atoms will break up. The probability of disintegration – in effect, the half-life – depends on the particular structure, In general, though, the higher the atomic number, the lower the stability.

Early researchers thought the natural series ended at uranium. If further elements had once existed, they had long since perished. Neptunium, plutonium, and the rest must be made artificially. Later, traces of them were found in nature; but merely traces, and only of nuclei whose atomic numbers were below 100. The creation of new substances grew progressively more difficult, because of proton repulsion, and less rewarding, because of vanishingly brief existence, as atomic number increased. Few people expected a figure as high as 120 would ever be reached.

Well, few people expected gravity control or faster-than-light travel, either. The universe is rather bigger and more complicated than any given set of brains. Already in those days, an astonishing truth was soon revealed. Beyond a certain point, nuclei become *more* stable. The periodic table contains an 'island of stability', bounded on the near side by ghostly short-lived isotopes like those of 112 and 113, on the far side by the still more speedily fragmenting 123, 124 . . . etc . . . on to the next 'island' which theory says could exist but practice has not reached save on the most infinitesimal scale.

The first is amply hard to attain. There are no easy intermediate stages, like the neptunium which is a stage between uranium and plutonium. Beyond 100, a half-life of a few hours is Methuselan; most are measured in seconds or less. You build your nuclei by main force, slamming particles into atoms too hard for them to rebound – though not so hard that the targets shatter.

To make a few micrograms of, say, element 114, eka-platinum, was a laboratory triumph. Aside from knowledge gained, it had no industrial meaning.

Engineers grew wistful about that. The proper isotope of eka-platinum will not endure forever; yet its half-life is around a quarter million years, abundant for mortal purposes, a radioactivity too weak to demand special precautions. It is lustrous white, dense (31.7), of high melting point (ca. 4700°C.), nontoxic, hard and tough and resistant. You can only get it into solution by grinding it to dust, then treating it with H_2F_2 and fluorine gas, under pressure at 250°.

It can alloy to produce metals with a range of properties an engineer would scarcely dare daydream about. Or, pure, used as a catalyst, it can become a veritable Philosopher's Stone. Its neighbors on the island are still more fascinating.

When Satan was discovered, talk arose of large-scale manufacture. Calculations soon damped it. The mills which were being designed would use rivers and seas and an entire atmosphere for cooling, whole continents for dumping wastes, in producing special isotopes by the ton. But these isotopes would all belong to elements below 100. Not even on Satan could modern technology handle the energies involved in creating, within reasonable time, a ton of eka-platinum; and supposing this were somehow possible, the cost would remain out of anybody's reach.

The engineers sighed ... until a new company appeared, offering supermetals by the ingot or the shipload, at prices high but economic. The source of supply was not revealed. Governments and the Council of the League remembered the Shenna.

To them, a Cynthian named Tso Yu explained blandly that the organization for which she spoke had developed a new process which it chose not to patent but to keep proprietary. Obviously, she said, new laws of nature had been discovered first; but Supermetals felt no obligation to publish for the benefit of science. Let science do its own sweating. Nor did her company wish to join the League, or put itself under any government. If some did not grant it license to operate in their territories, why, there was no lack of others who would.

In the three years since, engineers had begun doing things and building devices which were to bring about the same kind of revolution as did the transistor, the fusion converter, or the negagravity generator. Meanwhile a horde of investigators, public and private, went quietly frantic.

The crews who delivered the cargoes and the agents who sold them were a mixed lot, albeit of known species. A high proportion were from backward worlds like Diomedes, Woden, or Ikrananka; some originated in neglected colonies like Lochlann (human) or Catawrayannis (Cynthian). This was understandable. Beings to whom Supermetals had given an education and a chance to better themselves and help out their folk at home would be especially loyal to it. Enough employees hailed from sophisticated milieus to deal on equal terms with League executives.

This did not appear to be a Shenn situation. Whenever an individual's past life could be traced, it proved normal, up to the point when Supermetals engaged him (her, it, yx . . .) – and was not really abnormal now. Asked point blank, the being would say he didn't know himself where the factory was or how it functioned or who the ultimate owners were. He was merely doing a well-paid job for a good, *simpático* outfit. The evidence bore him out.

('I suspect, me, some detecting was done by kidnaps, drugs, and afterward murder,' van Rijn said bleakly. 'I would never allow that, but fact is, a few Supermetals people have disappeared. And . . . as youngsters like you,

Coya, get more prudish, the companies and governments get more brutish.' She answered: 'The second is part of the reason for the first.')

Scoutships trailed the carriers and learned that they always rendezvoused with smaller craft, built for speed and agility. Three or four of these would unload into a merchantman, then dash off in unpredictable directions, using every evasive maneuver in the book and a few that the League had thought were its own secrets. They did not stop dodging until their instruments confirmed that they had shaken their shadowers.

Politicians and capitalists alike organized expensive attempts to duplicate the discoveries of whoever was behind Supermetals. Thus far, progress was nil. A body of opinion grew, that that order of capabilities belonged to a society as far ahead of the Technic as the latter was ahead of the neolithic. Then why this quiet invasion?

'I'm surprised nobody but you has thought of the supernova alternative,' Coya said.

'Well, it *has* barely been three years,' van Rijn answered. 'And the business began small. It is still not big. Nothing flashy-splashy: some kilotons arriving annually, of stuff what is useful and will get more useful after more is learned about the properties. Meanwhiles, everybody got lots else to think about, the usual skulduggeries and unknowns and whatnots. Finalwise, remember, I am pustulent – *dood en ondergang*, this Anglic! – I am postulating something which astronomically is hyperimprobable. If you asked a colleague offhand, his first response would be that it isn't possible. His second would be, if he is a sensible man, How would you like to come to his place for a drink?' He knocked the dottle from his pipe. 'No doubt somebody more will eventual think of it too, and sic a computer onto the problem of: Is this sort of thing possible, and if so, where might we find one?'

He stroked his goatee. 'Howsomever,' he continued musingly, 'I think a good whiles must pass before the idea does occur. You see, the ordinary being does not care. He buys from what is on the market without wondering where it come from or what it means. Besides, Supermetals has not gone after publicity, it uses direct contacts; and what officials are concerned about Supermetals has been happy to avoid publicity themselves. A big harroo might too easy get out of control, lose them votes or profits or something.'

'Nevertheless,' Coya said, 'a number of bright minds are worrying; and the number grows as the amount of supermetals brought in does.'

'*Ja*. Except who wears those minds? Near-as-damn all is corporation executives, politicians, laboratory scientists, military officers, and – now I will have to wash my mouth out with Genever – bureaucrats. In shorts, they is planet-lubbers. When they cross space, they go by cozy passenger ships, to cities where everything is known except where is a restaurant fit to eat in that don't charge as if the dessert was eka-platinum à la mode.

'Me, my first jobs was on prospecting voyages. And I traveled plenty after I founded Solar, troublepotshooting on the frontier and beyond in my own personals. I know – every genuine spaceman knows, down in his marrow like no deskman ever can – how God always makes surprises on us so we don't get too proud, or maybe just for fun. To me it came natural to ask myself: What joke might God have played on the theorists this time?'

'I hope it is only a joke,' Coya said.

The star remained a titan in mass. In dimensions, it was hardly larger than Earth, and shrinking still, megayear by megayear, until at last light itself could no longer escape and there would be in the universe one more point of elemental blackness and strangeness. That process was scarcely started – Coya estimated the explosion had occurred some 500 millennia ago – and the giant-become-dwarf radiated dimly in the visible spectrum, luridly in the X-ray and gamma bands. That is, each square centimeter emitted a gale of hard quanta; but so small was the area in interstellar space that the total was a mere spark, undetectable unless you came within a few parsecs.

Standing in the observation turret, staring into a view-screen set for maximum photoamplification, she discerned a wan-white speck amidst stars which thronged the sky and, themselves made to seem extra brilliant, hurt her eyes. She looked away, toward the instruments around her which were avidly gathering data. The ship whispered and pulsed, no longer under hyperdrive but accelerating on negagravity thrust.

Hirharouk's voice blew cool out of the intercom, from the navigation bridge where he was: 'The existence of a companion is now confirmed. We will need a long baseline to establish its position, but preliminary indications are of a radius vector between forty and fifty a.u.'

Coya marveled at a detection system which could identify the light-bending due to a substellar object at that distance. Any observatory would covet such equipment. Her thought went to van Rijn: *If you paid what it cost, Gunung Tuan, you were smelling big money.*

'So far?' came her grandfather's words. 'By damn, a chilly ways out, enough to freeze your astronomy off.'

'It had to be,' she said. 'This was an A-zero: radiation equal to a hundred Sols. Closer in, even a superjovian would have been cooked down to the bare metal – as happened when the sun detonated.'

'*Ja*, I knows, I knows, my dear. I only did not foresee things here was on quite this big a scale . . . Well, we can't spend weeks at sublight. Go hyper, Hirharouk, first to get your baseline sights, next to come near the planet.'

'Hyperdrive, this deep in a gravitational well?' Coya exclaimed.

'Is hokay if you got good engines well tuned, and you bet ours is tuned like a late Beethoven quartet. Music, maestro!'

Coya shook her head before she prepared to continue gathering information under the new conditions of travel.

Again *Dewfall* ran on gravs. Van Rijn agreed that trying to pass within visual range of the ultimate goal, faster than light, when to them it was still little more than a mystery wrapped in conjectures, would be a needlessly expensive form of suicide.

Standing on the command bridge between him and Hirharouk, Coya stared at the meters and displays filling an entire bulkhead, as if they could tell more than the heavens in the screens. And they could, they could, but they were not the Earth-built devices she had been using; they were Ythrian and she did not know how to read them.

Poised on his perch, crested carnivore head lifted against the Milky Way, Hirharouk said: 'Data are pouring in as we approach. We should make optical pickup in less than an hour.'

'Hum-hum, better call battle stations,' the man proposed.

'This crew needs scant notice. Let them slake any soul-thirst they feel. God may smite some of us this day.' Through the intercom keened a melody, plangent strings and thuttering drums and shrilling pipes, like nothing Earth had brought forth but still speaking to Coya of hunters high among their winds.

Terror stabbed her. 'You can't expect to fight!' she cried.

'Oh, an ordinary business precaution,' van Rijn smiled.

'No! We mustn't!'

'Why not, if they are here and do rumblefumbles at us?'

She opened her lips, pulled them shut again, and stood in anguish. *I can't tell you why not. How can I tell you these may be David's people?*

'At least we are sure that Supermetals is not a *whinna* for an alien society,' Hirharouk said. Coya remembered vaguely, through the racket in her temples, a demonstration of the *whinna* during her groundside visit to Ythri. It was a kind of veil, used by some to camouflage themselves, to resemble floating mists in the eyes of unflying prey; and this practical use had led to a form of dreamlovely airborne dance; and – *And here I was caught in the wonder of what we have found, a thing which must be almost unique even in this galaxy full of miracles . . . and everything's gotten tangled and ugly and, and, David what can we do?*

She heard van Rijn: 'Well, we are not total-sure. Could be our finding is accidental; or maybe the planet is not like we suppose. We got to check on that, and hope the check don't bounce back in our snoots.'

'Nuclear engines are in operation around our quarry,' Hirharouk said. 'Neutrinos show it. What else would they belong to save a working base and spacecraft?'

Van Rijn clasped hands over rump and paced, slap-slap-slap over the bare deck. 'What can we try and predict in advance? Forewarned is forearmed, they say, and the four arms I want right now is a knife, a blaster, a machine gun, and a rover missile, nothing fancy, maybe a megaton.'

'The mass of the planet – ' Hirharouk consulted a readout. The figure he gave corresponded approximately to Saturn.

'No bigger?' asked van Rijn, surprised.

'Originally, yes,' Coya heard herself say. The scientist in her was what spoke, while her heart threshed about like any animal netted by a stooping Ythrian. 'A gas giant, barely substellar. The supernova blew most of that away – you can hardly say it boiled the gases off; we have no words for what happened – and nothing was left except a core of nickel-iron and heavier elements.'

She halted, noticed Hirharouk's yellow gaze intent on her, and realized the skipper must know rather little of the theory behind this venture. To him she had not been repeating banalities. And he was interested. If she could please him by explaining in simple terms, then maybe later –

She addressed him: 'Of course, when the pressure of the outer layers was removed, that core must have exploded into new allotropes, a convulsion which flung away the last atmosphere and maybe a lot of solid matter. Better keep a sharp lookout for meteoroids.'

'That is automatic,' he assured her. 'My wonder is why a planet should exist. I was taught that giant stars, able to become supernovae, do not have them.'

'Well, they is still scratching their brains to account for Betelgeuse,' van Rijn remarked.

'In this case,' Coya told the Ythrian, 'the explanation comes easier. True, the extremely massive suns do not in general allow planetary systems to condense around them. The parameters aren't right. However, you know giants can be partners in multiple star systems, and sometimes the difference between partners is quite large. So, after I was alerted to the idea that it might happen, and wrote a program which investigated the possibility in detail, I learned that, yes, under special conditions, a double can form in which one member is a large sun and one a super-jovian planet. When I extrapolated backward things like the motion of dust and gas, changes in galactic magne-

130

tism, et cetera – it turned out that such a pair could exist in this neighborhood.'

Her glance crossed the merchant's craggy features. *You found a clue in the appearance of the supermetals,* she thought. *David got the idea all by himself.* The lean snub-nosed face, the Vega-blue eyes came between her and the old man.

Of course, David may not have been involved. This could be a coincidence. Please, God of my grandfather Whom I don't believe in, please make it a coincidence. Make those ships ahead of us belong not to harmless miners but to the great and terrible Elder Race.

She knew the prayer would not be granted. And neither van Rijn nor Hirharouk assumed that the miners were necessarily harmless.

She talked fast, to stave off silence: 'I daresay you've heard this before, Captain, but you may like to have me recapitulate in a few words. When a supernova erupts, it floods out neutrons in quantities that I, I can put a number to, perhaps, but I cannot comprehend. In a full range of energies, too, and the same for other kinds of particles and quanta – Do you see? Any possible reaction *must* happen.

'Of course, the starting materials available, the reaction rates, the yields, every quantity differs from case to case. The big nuclei which get formed, like the actinides, are a very small percentage of the total. The supermetals are far less. They scatter so thinly into space that they're effectively lost. No detectable amount enters into the formation of a star or planet afterward.

'Except – here – here was a companion, a planet-sized companion, turned into a bare metallic globe. I wouldn't try to guess how many quintillion tons of blasted-out incandescent gases washed across it. Some of those alloyed with the molten surface, maybe some plated out

131

– and the supermetals, with their high condensation temperatures, were favored.

'A minute fraction of the total was supermetals, yes, and a minute fraction of that was captured by the planet, also yes. But this amounted to – how much? – billions of tons? Not hard to extract from combination by modern methods; and a part may actually be lying around pure. It's radioactive; one must be careful, especially of the shorter-lived products, and a lot has decayed away by now. Still, what's left is more than our puny civilization can ever consume. It took a genius to think this might be!'

She grew aware of van Rijn's eyes upon her. He had stopped pacing and stood troll-burly, tugging his beard.

A whistle rescued her. Planha words struck from the intercom. Hirharouk's feathers rippled in a series of expressions she could not read; his tautness was unmistakable.

She drew near to the man's bulk. 'What next?' she whispered. 'Can you follow what they're saying?'

'*Ja*, pretty well; anyhow, better than I can follow words in an opera. Detectors show three ships leaving planetary orbit on an intercept course. The rest stay behind. No doubt those is the working vessels. What they send to us is their men-of-war.'

Seen under full screen magnification, the supermetal world showed still less against the constellations than had the now invisible supernova corpse – a ball, dimly reflecting star-glow, its edge sharp athwart distant brightnesses. And yet, Coya thought: a world.

It could not be a smooth sphere. There must be uplands, lowlands, flatlands, depths, ranges and ravines, cliffs whose gloom was flecked with gold, plains where mercury glaciers glimmered; there must be internal heat, shudders in the steel soil, volcanoes spouting forth flame and radioactive ash; eternally barren, it must nonetheless mumble with a life of its own.

Had David Falkayn trod those lands? He would have, she knew, merrily swearing because beyond the ship's generated field he and his space gear weighed five or six times what they ought, and no matter the multitudinous death traps which a place so uncanny must hold in every shadow. Naturally, those shadows had to be searched out; whoever would mine the metals had first to spend years, and doubtless lives, in exploring, and studying, and the development and testing and redevelopment of machinery ... but that wouldn't concern David. He was a charger, not a plowhorse. Having made his discovery, told chosen beings about it, perhaps helped them raise the initial funds and recruit members of races which could better stand high weight than men can – having done that, he'd depart on a new adventure, or stop off in the Solar Commonwealth and take Coya Conyon out dancing.

'*Iyan wherill-ll cha quellan.*'

The words, and Hirharouk's response, yanked her back to this instant. 'What?'

'Shush.' Van Rijn, head cocked, waved her to silence. 'By damn, this sounds spiky. I should tell you, Shush-kebab.'

Hirharouk related: 'Instruments show one of the three vessels is almost equal to ours. Its attendants are less, but in a formation to let them take full advantage of their firepower. If that is in proportion to size, which I see no reason to doubt, we are outgunned. Nor do they act as if they simply hope to frighten us off. That formation and its paths are well calculated to bar our escape spaceward.'

'Can you give me details – ? No, wait.' Van Rijn swung on Coya. 'Bellybird, you took a stonkerish lot of readings on the sun, and right here is an input-output panel you

133

can switch to the computer system you was using. I also ordered, when I chartered the ship, should be a program for instant translation between Anglic language, Arabic numerals, metric units, whatever else kinds of ics is useful – translations back and forth between those and the Planha sort. Think you could quick-like do some figuring for us?' He clapped her shoulder, nearly felling her. 'I know you can.' His voice dropped. 'I remember your grandmother.'

Her mouth was dry, her palms were wet, it thudded in her ears. She thought of David Falkayn and said, 'Yes. What do you want?'

'Mainly the pattern of the gravitational field, and what phenomena we can expect at the different levels of intensity. Plus radiation, electromagnetics, anything else you got time to program for. But we is fairly well protected against those, so don't worry if you don't get a chance to go into details there. Nor don't let outside talkings distract you – Whoops!' Hirharouk was receiving a fresh report. 'Speak of the devil and he gives you horns.'

The other commander had obviously sent a call on a standard band, which had been accepted. As the image screen awoke, Coya felt hammerstruck. *Adzel!*

No . . . no . . . the head belonged to a Wodenite, but not the dear dragon who had given her rides on his back when she was little and had tried in his earnest, tolerant fashion to explain his Buddhism to her when she grew older. Behind the being she made out a raven-faced Ikranankan and a human in the garb of a colony she couldn't identify.

His rubbery lips shaped good Anglic, a basso which went through her bones: 'Greeting. Commodore Nadi speaks.'

Van Rijn thrust his nose toward the scanner. 'Whose

134

commodore?' he demanded like a gravel hauler dumping its load.

For a second, Nadi was shaken. He rallied and spoke firmly: '*Kho*, I know who you are, Freeman van Rijn. What an unexpected honor, that you should personally visit our enterprise.'

'Which is Supermetals, *nie*?'

'It would be impolite to suggest you had failed to reach that conclusion.'

Van Rijn signalled Coya behind his back. She flung herself at the chair before the computer terminal. Hirharouk perched imperturbable, slowly fanning his wings. The Ythrian music had ended. She heard a rustle and whisper through the intercom, along the hurtling hull.

Words continued. Her work was standardized enough that she could follow them.

'Well, you see, Commodore, there I sat, not got much to do no more, lonely old man like I am except when a girl goes wheedle-wheedle at me, plenty time for thinking, which is not fun like drinking but you can do it alone and it is easier on the kidneys and the hangovers next day are not too much worse. I thought, if the supermetals is not made by an industrial process we don't understand, must be they was made by a natural one, maybe one we do know a little about. That would have to be a supernova. Except a supernova blows everything out into space, and the supermetals is so small, proportional, that they get lost. Unless the supernova had a companion what could catch them?'

'Freeman, pray accept my admiration. Does your perspicacity extend to deducing who is behind our undertaking?'

'*Ja*, I can say, bold and bald, who you undertakers are. A consortium of itsy-bitsy operators, most from poor or primitive societies, pooling what capital they can scrape

135

together. You got to keep the secret, because if they know about this hoard you found, the powerful outfits will horn themselves in and you out; and what chance you get afterward, in courts they can buy out of petty cash? No, you will keep this hidden long as you possible can. In the end, somebody is bound to repeat my sherlockery. But give you several more years, and you will have pumped gigacredits clear profit out of here. You may actual have got so rich you can defend your property.'

Coya could all but see the toilers in their darkness – in orbital stations; aboard spacecraft; down on the graveyard surface, where robots dug ores and ran refineries, and sentient beings stood their watches under the murk and chill and weight and radiation and millionfold perils of Eka-World . . .

Nadi, slow and soft: 'That is why we have these fighting ships, Freeman and Captain.'

'You do not suppose,' van Rijn retorted cheerily, 'I would come this far in my own precious blubber and forget to leave behind a message they will scan if I am not home in time to race for the Micronesia Cup?'

'As a matter of fact, Freeman, I suppose precisely that. The potential gains here are sufficient to justify virtually any risk, whether the game be played for money or . . . something else.' Pause. 'If you have indeed left a message, you will possess hostage value. Your rivals may be happy to see you a captive, but you have allies and employees who will exert influence. My sincere apologies, Freeman, Captain, everyone aboard your vessel. We will try to make your detention pleasant.'

Van Rijn's bellow quivered in the framework. '*Wat drommel?* You sit smooth and calm like buttered granite and say you will make us prisoners?'

'You may not leave. If you try, we will regretfully open fire.'

'You are getting on top of yourself. I warn you, always she finds nothing except an empty larder, Old Mother Hubris.'

'Freeman, please consider. We noted your hyperdrive vibrations and made ready. You cannot get past us to spaceward. Positions and vectors guarantee that one of our vessels will be able to close in, engage, and keep you busy until the other two arrive.' Reluctantly, van Rijn nodded. Nadi continued: 'True, you can double back toward the sun. Evidently you can use hyperdrive closer to it than most. But you cannot go in that direction at anywhere near top pseudospeed without certain destruction. We, proceeding circuitously, but therefore able to go a great deal faster, will keep ahead of you. We will calculate the conoid in which your possible paths spaceward lie, and again take a formation you cannot evade.'

'You is real anxious we should taste your homebrew, ha?'

'Freeman, I beg you, yield at once. I promise fair treatment – if feasible, compensation – and while you are among us, I will explain why we of Supermetals have no choice.'

'Hirharouk,' van Rijn said, 'maybe you can talk at this slagbrain.' He stamped out of scanner reach. The Ythrian threw him a dubious glance but entered into debate with the Wodenite. Van Rijn hulked over Coya where she sat. 'How you coming?' he whispered, no louder than a Force Five wind.

She gestured at the summary projected on a screen. Her computations were of a kind she often handled. The results were shown in such terms as diagrams and equations of equipotential surfaces, familiar to a space captain. Van Rijn read them and nodded. 'We got enough information to set out on,' he decided. 'The rest you can figure while we go.'

Shocked, she gaped at him. 'What? Go? But we're caught!'

'He thinks that. Me, I figured whoever squats on a treasure chest will keep guards, and the guards will not be glimmerwits but smart, trained oscos, in spite of what I called the Commodore. They might well cook for us a cake like what we is now baked in. Ergo, I made a surprise recipe for them.' Van Rijn's regard turned grave. 'It was for use only if we found we was sailing through dire straits. The surprise may turn around and bite us. Then we is dead. But better dead than losing years in the nicest jail, *nie*?' (And she could not speak to him of David.) 'I said this trip might be dangerous.' Enormous and feathergentle, a hand stroked down her hair. 'I is very sorry, Beatriz, Ramona.' The names he murmured were of her mother and grandmother.

Whirling, he returned to Hirharouk, who matched pride against Nadi's patience, and uttered a few rapid-fire Planha words. The Ythrian gave instant assent. Suddenly Coya knew why the man had chosen a ship of that planet. Hirharouk continued his argument. Van Rijn went to the main command panel, snapped forth orders, and took charge of *Dewfall*.

At top acceleration, she sprang back toward the sun.

Of that passage, Coya afterward remembered little. First she glimpsed the flashes when nuclear warheads drove at her, and awaited death. But van Rijn and Hirharouk had adjusted well their vector relative to the enemy's. During an hour of negagrav flight, no missile could gather sufficient relative velocity to get past defensive fire; and that was what made those flames in heaven.

Then it became halfway safe to go hyper. That must be at a slower pace than in the emptiness between stars; but within an hour, the fleeing craft neared the dwarf. There, as gravitation intensified, she had to resume normal state.

Instead of swinging wide, she opened full thrust almost straight toward the disc.

Coya was too busy to notice much of what happened around her. She must calculate, counsel, hang into her seat harness as forces tore at her which were too huge for the compensator fields. She saw the undead supernova grow in the viewscreens till its baneful radiance filled them; she heard the ribs of the vessel groan and felt them shudder beneath stress; she watched the tale of the radiation meters mounting and knew how close she came to a dose whose ravages medicine could not heal; she heard orders bawled by van Rijn, fluted by Hirharouk, and whistling replies and storm of wingbeats, always triumphant though *Dewfall* flew between the teeth of destruction. But mainly she was part of the machinery.

And the hours passed and the hours passed.

They could not have done what they did without advance preparation. Van Rijn had foreseen the contingency and ordered computations made whose results were in the data banks. Her job was to insert numbers and functions corresponding to the reality on hand, and get answers by which he and Hirharouk might steer. The work filled her, crowded out terror and sometimes the memory of David.

Appalled, Nadi watched his quarry vanish off his telltales. He had followed on hyperdrive as close as he dared, and afterward at sublight closer than he ought to have dared. But for him was no possibility of plunging in a hairpin hyperbola around yonder incandescence. In all the years he had been stationed here, not he nor his fellows had imagined anyone would ever venture near the roiling remnant of a sun which had once burned brighter than its whole galaxy. Thus there were no precalculations in storage, nor days granted him to program them on a larger device than a ship might carry.

Radiation was not the barrier. It was easy to figure how narrow an approach a crew could endure behind a given amount of armor. But a mass of half a dozen Sols, pressed into the volume of an Earth, has stupendous gravitational power; the warped space around makes the laws of nature take on an eerie aspect. Moreover, a dwarf star spins at a fantastic rate: which generates relativistic forces, describable only if you have determined the precise quantities involved. And pulsations, normally found nowhere outside the atomic nucleus, reach across a million or more kilometers –

After the Ythrian craft whipped around the globe, into weirdness, Nadi had no way of knowing what she did, how she moved. He could not foretell where she would be when she again became detectable. And thus he could plan no interception pattern.

He could do nothing but hope she would never reappear. A ship flying so close, not simply orbiting but flying, would be seized, torn apart, and hauled into the star, unless the pilot and his computers knew exactly what they did.

Or almost exactly. That was a crazily chancy ride. When Coya could glance from her desk, she saw blaze in the screens, Hirharouk clutching his perch with both hands while his wings thundered and he yelled for joy, van Rijn on his knees in prayer. Then they ran into a meteoroid swarm (she supposed) which rebounded off their shieldfields and sent them careening off trajectory; and the man shook his fist, commenced on a mighty oath, glimpsed her and turned it into a Biblical 'Damask rose and shittah tree!' Later, when something else went wrong – some interaction with a plasma cloud – he came to her, bent over and kissed her brow.

They won past reef and riptide, lined out for deep

140

space, switched back into hyperdrive and ran on home-ward.

Coincidences do happen. The life would be freakish which held none of them.

Muddlin' Through, bound for Eka-World in response to Coya's letter, passed within detection range of *Dewfall*, made contact, and laid alongside. The pioneers boarded.

This was less than a day after the brush with oblivion. And under no circumstances do Ythrians go in for tumultuous greetings. Apart from Hirharouk, who felt he must represent his choth, the crew stayed at rest. Coya, roused by van Rijn, swallowed a stimpill, dressed, and hastened to the flying hold – the sole chamber aboard which would comfortably accommodate Adzel. In its echoing dim space she threw her arms partway around him, took Chee Lan into her embrace, kissed David Falkayn and wept and kissed him and kissed him.

Van Rijn cleared his throat. 'A-hem!' he grumbled. 'Also bgr-rrm. I been sitting here hours on end, till my end is sore, wondering when everybody elses would come awake and make celebrations by me; and I get word about you three mosquito-ears is coming in, and by my own self I hustle stuff for a party.' He waved at the table he had laid, bottles and glasses, platesful of breads, cheeses, sausage, lox, caviar, kanuba, from somewhere a vaseful of flowers. Mozart lilted in the background. 'Well, ha, poets tell us love is enduring, but I tell us good food is not, so we take our funs in the right order, *nie*?'

Formerly Falkayn would have laughed and tossed off the first icy muglet of akvavit; he would have followed it with a beer chaser and an invitation to Coya that they see what they could dance to this music. Now she felt sinews tighten in the fingers that enclosed hers; across her shoulder he said carefully: 'Sir, before we relax, could you let me know what's happened to you?'

Van Rijn got busy with a cigar. Coya looked a plea at Adzel, stroked Chee's fur where the Cynthian crouched on a chair, and found no voice. Hirharouk told the story in a few sharp words.

'A-a-ah,' Falkayn breathed. 'Judas priest. Coya, they ran you that close to that hellkettle – ' His right hand let go of hers to clasp her waist. She felt the grip tremble and grew dizzy with joy.

'Well,' van Rijn huffed, 'I didn't want she should come, my dear tender little bellybird, *ja*, tender like tool steel – '

Coya had a sense of being put behind Falkayn, as a man puts a woman when menace draws near. 'Sir,' he said most levelly, 'I know, or can guess, about that. We can discuss it later if you want. What I'd like to know immediately, please, is what you propose to do about the Supermetals consortium.'

Van Rijn kindled his cigar and twirled a mustache. 'You understand,' he said, 'I am not angry if they keep things under the posies. By damn, though, they tried to make me a prisoner or else shoot me to bits of lard what would go into the next generation of planets. And Coya, too, Davy boy, don't forget Coya, except she would make those planets prettier. For that, they going to pay.'

'What have you in mind?'

'Oh . . . a cut. Not the most unkindest, neither. Maybe like ten percent of gross.'

The creases deepened which a hundred suns had weathered into Falkayn's countenance. 'Sir, you don't need the money. You stopped needing more money a long while back. To you it's nothing but a counter in a game. Maybe, for you, the only game in town. Those beings aft of us, however – they are not playing.'

'What do they do, then?'

Surprisingly, Hirharouk spoke. 'Freeman, you know the answer. They seek to win that which will let their peoples fly free.' Standing on his wings, he could not spread gold-bronze plumes, but his head rose high. 'In the end, God the Hunter strikes every being and everything which beings have made. Upon your way of life I see His shadow. Let the new come to birth in peace.'

From Falkayn's hands, Coya begged: '*Gunung Tuan*, all you have to do is do nothing. Say nothing. You've won your victory. Tell them that's enough for you, that you too are their friend.'

She had often watched van Rijn turn red – never before white. His shout came ragged: '*Ja! Ja!* Friend! So nice, so kind, maybe so farsighted – Who, what I thought of like a son, broke his oath of fealty to me? Who broke kinship?'

He suspected, Coya realized sickly, *but he wouldn't admit it to himself till this minute, when I let out the truth.* She held Falkayn sufficiently hard for everyone to see.

Chee Lan arched her back. Adzel grew altogether still. Falkayn forgot Coya – she could feel how he did – and looked straight at his chief while he said, word by word like blows of a hammer: 'Do you want a response? I deem best we let what is past stay dead.'

Their gazes drew apart. Falkayn's dropped to Coya. The merchant watched them standing together for a soundless minute. And upon him were the eyes of Adzel, Chee, and Hirharouk the sky dweller.

He shook his head. 'Hokay,' said Nicholas van Rijn, well-nigh too low to hear. 'I keep my mouth shut. Always. Now can we sit down and have our party for making you welcome?' He moved to pour from a bottle; and Coya saw that he was indeed old.

The rest would appear to be everyone's knowledge: how at last, inevitably, the secret of Mirkheim's existence was ripped asunder; how the contest for its possession brought on the Babur War; how that struggle turned out to be the first civil war in the Commonwealth and gave the Polesotechnic League a mortal wound. The organization would linger on for another hundred Terran years, but waning and disintegrating; in truth, already it had ceased to be what it began as, the proud upbearer of liberty. Eventually the Commonwealth, too, went under. The Troubles were only quelled with the rise and expansion of the Empire – and its interior peace is often bought with foreign violence, as Ythri and Avalon have learned. Honor be forever theirs whose deathpride preserved for us our right to rule ourselves!

Surely much of that spirit flies through time from David and Coya Conyon/Falkayn. When they led to this planet humans who would found new homes, they were doing more than escaping from the chaos they foresaw; they were raising afresh the ancient banner of freedom. When they obtained the protection and cooperation of Ythri, they knew – it is in their writings – how rich and strong a world must come from the dwelling together of two races so unlike.

Thus far the common wisdom. As for the creation and history of our choth upon Avalon, that is in *The Sky Book of Stormgate.*

Yet Hloch has somewhat more to give you before his own purpose is fully served. As you well know, our unique society did not come easily into being. Especially in the early years, misunderstandings, conflicts, bitterness, even enmity would often strike talons into folk. Have you heard much of this from the human side? Belike not. It is fitting that you learn.

Hloch has therefore chosen two final tales as representative. That they are told from youthful hoverpoints is, in his mind, very right.

The first of them is the last that Judith Dalmady/ Lundgren wrote for *Morgana.* Though she was then in her high old age, the memories upon which she was drawing were fresh.

As far as we know – but how much do we really know, in this one corner of this one galaxy which we have somewhat explored? – Avalon was the first planet whereon two different intelligent species founded a joint colony. Thus much was unforeseeable, not only about the globe itself, whose mysteries had barely been skimmed by the original explorers, but about the future of so mixed a people. The settlers began by establishing themselves in the Hesperian Islands, less likely to hold fatal surprises than a continent. And the two races chose different territories.

Relations between them were cordial, of course. Both looked forward to the day when men and Ythrians would take over the mainlands and dwell there together. But at first it seemed wise to avoid possible friction. After all, they had scarcely anything in common except more or less similar biochemistries, warm blood, live birth, and the hope of making a fresh start on an uncorrupted world. Let them get acquainted gradually, let mutuality develop in an unforced way.

Hence Nat Falkayn rarely saw winged folk in the early part of his life. When an Ythrian did, now and then, have business in Chartertown, it was apt to be with his grandfather David, or, presently, his father Nicholas: certainly not with a little boy. Even when an eaglelike being came as a dinner guest, conversation was seldom in Anglic. Annoyed by this, Nat grew downright grindstone about learning the Planha language as his school required. But the effort didn't pay off until he was seventeen Avalonian years old – twelve years of that Mother Earth he had never seen, of which his body bore scarcely an atom.

At that time, the archipelago settlements had grown to a point where leaders felt ready to plant a seed of habitation on the Coronan continent. But much study and planning must go before. Nicholas Falkayn, an engineer, was among those humans who joined Ythrian colleagues in a research and development team. The headquarters of his happened to be at the chief abode of the allied folk, known to its dwellers as Trauvay and to humans as Wingland. He would be working out of there for many cycles of the moon Morgana, each of which equalled not quite half a Lunar month. So he brought his wife and children along.

Nat found himself the only boy around in his own age bracket. However, there was no lack of young Ythrian companions.

'Hyaa-aah!' In a whirl and thunder, Keshchyi left the balcony floor and swung aloft. Sunlight blazed off his feathers. The whistling, trumpeting challenge blew down: 'What are you waiting for, you mudfeet?'

Less impetuous than his cousin, Thuriak gave Nat a sharp yellow glance. 'Well, are you coming?' he asked.

'I . . . guess so,' the human mumbled.

You are troubled, Thuriak said, not with his voice.

Infinitely variable, Ythrian plumage can send ripples of expression across the entire body, signs and symbols often more meaningful than words will ever be. Nat had learned some of the conventional attitudes as part of his Planha lessons. But now, during these days of real acquaintance with living creatures, he had come to feel more and more like a deaf-mute.

He could merely say, in clumsy direct speech: 'No, I'm fine. Honest I am. Just, uh, well, wondering if I shouldn't at least call my mother and ask – '

His tone trailed off. Thuriak seemed to be registering scorn. And yet this was a gentle, considerate youth, not at all like that overbearing Keshchyi . . .

If you must, like a nestling. Did that really stand written on the bronze-hued feathers, the black-edged white of crest and tail?

Nat felt very alone. He'd been delighted when these contemporaries of his, with whom he'd talked a bit and played a few games, invited him to spend the Freedom Week vacation at their home. And certainly that whole extended household known as the Weathermaker Choth had shown him politeness, if not intimacy – aside from a few jeering remarks of Keshchyi's, which the fellow probably didn't realize were painful. And his parents had been glad to let him accept. 'It's a step toward the future,' his father had exclaimed. 'Our two kinds are going to have to come to know each other inside out. That's a job for your generation, Nat . . . and here you're beginning on it.'

But the Ythrians were alien, and not just in their society. In their bones, their flesh, the inmost molecules of their genes, they were not human. It was no use pretending otherwise.

'Different' did not necessarily mean 'inferior'. Could it, heartbreakingly, mean 'better'? Or 'happier'? Had

God been in a more joyful mood when He made Ythrians than when He made man?

Perhaps not. They were pure carnivores, born hunters. Maybe that was the reason why they allowed, yes, encouraged their young to go off and do reckless things, accepting stoically the fact that the unfit and the unlucky would not return alive –

Keshchyi swooped near. Nat felt a gust of air from beneath his wings. 'Are you glued in your place?' he shouted. 'The tide isn't, I can tell you. If you want to come, then for thunder's sake, move!'

'He's right, you know,' said calmer Thuriak. Eagerness quivered across him.

Nat gulped. As if searching for something familiar, anything, his gaze swept around.

He stood on a balcony of that tall stone tower which housed the core families. Below were a paved courtyard and rambling wooden buildings. Meadows where meat animals grazed sloped downhill in Terrestrial grass and clover, Ythrian starbell and wry, Terrestrial oak and pine, Ythrian braidbark and copperwood, until cultivation gave way to the reddish mat of native susin, the scattered intense green of native chasuble bush and delicate blue of janie. The sun Laura stood big and golden-colored at morning, above a distantly glimpsed mercury line of ocean. Elsewhere wandered a few cottony clouds and the pale, sinking ghost of Morgana. A flock of Avalonian draculas passed across view, their leathery wings awkward beside the plumed splendor of Keshchyi's. No adult Ythrians were to be seen; they ranged afar on their business.

Nat, who was short and slender, with rumpled brown hair above thin feathers, felt dwarfed in immensity.

The wind murmured, caressed his face with coolness,

blew him an odor of leaves and distances, a smoky whiff of Thuriak's body.

Though young, that being stood nearly as tall as one full-grown, which meant that he was about Nat's height. What he stood on was his enormous wings, folded downward, claws at their main joints to serve as a kind of feet. What had been the legs and talons of his birdlike ancestors were, on him, arms and hands. His frame had an avian rigidity and jutting keelbone, but his head, borne proudly on a rather long neck, was almost mammalian beneath its crest – streamlined muzzle, tawny eyes, mouth whose lips looked oddly delicate against the fangs, little brow yet the skull bulging backward to hold an excellent brain.

'Are you off, then?' Thuriak demanded while Keshchyi whistled in heaven. 'Or would you rather stay here? It might be best for you, at that.'

Blood beat in Nat's temples. *I'm not going to let these creatures sneer at humans!* ran through him. At the same time he knew he was being foolish, that he ought to check with his mother – and knew he wasn't going to, that he couldn't help himself. 'I'm coming,' he snapped.

Good, said Thuriak's plumage. He brought his hands to the floor and stood on them an instant while he spread those wings. Light shining through made his pinions look molten. Beneath them, the gill-like antlibranch slits, the 'biological superchargers' which made it possible for an animal this size to fly under Earthlike conditions, gaped briefly, a row of purple mouths. In a rush and roar of his own, Thuriak mounted.

He swung in dizzying circles, up and up toward his hovering cousin. Shouts went between them. An Ythrian in flight burned more food and air than a human; they said he was more alive.

But I am no Ythrian, Nat thought. Tears stung him. He wiped them away, angrily, with the back of a wrist, and sought the controls of his gravbelt.

It encircled his coveralls at the waist. On his back were the two cylinders of its powerpack. He could rise, he could fly for hours. But how wretched a crutch this was!

Leaving the tower, he felt a slight steady vibration from the drive unit, pulsing through his belly. His fingers reached to adjust the controls, level him off and line him out northward. Wind blew, shrill and harsh, lashing his eyes till he must pull down the goggles on his leather helmet. The Ythrians had transparent third lids.

In the last several days, he had had borne in on him – until at night, on the cot set up for him in the young males' nest, he must stifle his sobs lest somebody hear – borne in on him how much these beings owned their unbounded skies, and how his kind did not.

The machine that carried him went drone, drone. He trudged on a straight course through the air, while his companions dipped and soared and reveled in the freedom of heaven which was their birthright.

The north shore curved to form a small bay. Beyond susin and bush and an arc of dunes, its waters glistened clear blue-green; surf roared furious on the reefs across its mouth. A few youngsters kept sailboats here. Keshchyi and Thuriak were among them.

But . . . they had quietly been modifying theirs for use on open sea. Today they proposed to take it out.

Nat felt less miserable when he had landed. On foot, he was the agile one, the Ythrians slow and limited. That was a poor tradeoff, he thought grayly. Still, he could be of help to them. Was that the real reason they had invited him to join this maiden venture?

For Keshchyi, yes, no doubt, the boy decided. *Thuriak seems to like me as a person . . . Seems* to. His look went across that haughty unhuman countenance, and though it was full of expression, he could read nothing more subtle than a natural excitement.

'Come on!' Keshchyi fairly danced in his impatience. 'Launch!' To Nat: 'You. Haul on the prow. We'll push on the stern. Jump!'

For a moment of anger, Nat considered telling him to go to hell and returning alone. He knew he wasn't supposed to be here anyway, on a dangerous faring, without háving so much as told his parents. The whole idea had been presented to him with such beast-of prey suddenness . . . *No*, he thought. *I can't let them believe I, a human, must be a coward. I'll show 'em better.* He seized the stempost, which curved over the bow in a graceful sculpture of vines and leaves. He bent his back and threw his muscles into work.

The boat moved readily from its shelter and across the beach. It was a slim, deckless, nearly flat-bottomed hull, carvel-built, about four meters long. A single mast rested in brackets. Sand, gritty beneath Nat's thin shoe-soles, gave way to a swirl of water around his trouser legs. The boat uttered a chuckling sound as it came afloat.

Keshchyi and Thuriak boarded in a single flap. Nat must make an undignified scramble across the gunwale and stand there dripping. Meanwhile the others raised the mast, secured its stays, began unlashing jib and mainsail. It was a curious rig, bearing a flexible gaff almost as long as the boom. The synthetic cloth rose crackling into the breeze.

'Hoy, wait a minute,' Nat said. The Ythrians gave him a blank glance and he realized he had spoken in Anglic. Had they never imagined it worth the trouble to learn his language properly, as he had theirs? He shifted to Planha: 'I've been sailing myself, around First Island, and know – uh, what is the word?' Flushing in embarrassment, he fumbled for ways to express his idea.

Thuriak helped him. After an effort, they reached understanding. 'You see we have neither keel nor centerboard, and wonder how we'll tack,' the Ythrian interpreted. 'I'm surprised the sportsmen of your race haven't adopted our design.' He swiveled a complexly curved board, self-adjusting on its pivot by means of vanes, upward from either rail. 'This interacts with the wind to provide lateral resistance. No water drag. Much faster than your craft. We'll actually sail as a hydrofoil.'

'Oh, grand!' Nat marvelled.

His pleasure soured when Keshchyi said in a patronizing tone: 'Well, of course, knowledge of the ways of air comes natural to us.'

'So we're off,' Thuriak laughed. He took the tiller in his right hand and jibsheet in his left; wing-claws gripped a perch-bar. The flapping sails drew taut. The boat bounded forward.

Hunkered in the bottom – there was no thwarts – Nat saw the waters swirl, heard them hiss, felt a shiver of speed and tasted salt on his lips. The boat reached planing speed and skimmed surface in a smooth gallop. The shore fell aft, the surf grew huge and loud ahead, dismayingly fast.

Nat gulped. *No, I will not show them any uneasiness.* After all, he still wore his gravbelt. In case of capsizing or – or whatever – he could flit to shore. The Ythrians could too. Was that why they didn't bother to carry lifejackets along?

The reefs were of some dark coraloid. They made a nearly unbroken low wall across the lagoon entrance. Breakers struck green-bright, smashed across those jagged backs, exploded in foam and bone-rattling thunder. Whirlpools seethed. In them, thick brown nets of atlantis weed, torn loose from a greater mass far out to sea, snaked around and around. Squinting through spindrift,

Nat barely made out a narrow opening toward which Thuriak steered.

I don't like this, I don't like it one bit, went through him, chill amidst primal bellows and grunts and hungry suckings.

Thuriak put down the helm. The boat came about in a slash of boom and gaff, a snap of sailcloth, sounds that were buried in the tornado racket. On its new tack, it leaped for the passage. Thuriak fluted his joy. Keshchyi spread plumes which shone glorious in sun and scud-blizzard.

The boat dived in among the reefs. An unseen net of weed caught the rudder. A riptide and a flaw of wind grabbed hold. The hull smashed against a ridge. Sharpnesses went like saws through the planks. The surf took the boat and started battering it to death.

Nat was aloft before he knew what had really happened. He hovered on his thrust-fields, above white and green violence, and stared wildly around. There was Thuriak, riding the air currents, dismay on every feather, but alive, safe . . . Where was Keshchyi?

Nat yelled the question. Faint through the noise there drifted back to him the shriek: 'I don't know, I don't see him, did the gaff whip over him – ?' and Thuriak swooped about and about, frantic.

A cry tore from him. 'Yonder!' And naked grief: 'No no, oh, Keshchyi, my blood-kin, my friend –'

Nat darted to join the Ythrian. Winds clawed at him; the breakers filled his head with their rage. Through a bitter upflung mist he peered. And he saw –

– Keshchyi, one wing tangled in the twining weed, a-thresh in waves that surged across him, bore him under, cast him back for an instant and swept him bloodily along a reefside.

'We can grab him!' Nat called. But he saw what

Thuriak had already seen, that this was useless. The mat which gripped Keshchyi was a dozen meters long and wide. It must weigh a ton or worse. He could not be raised, unless someone got in the water first to free him.

And Ythrians, winged sky-folk, plainly could not swim. It was flatout impossible for them. At most, help from above would keep the victim alive an extra minute or two.

Nat plunged.

Chaos closed on him. He had taken a full breath, and held it as he was hauled down into ice-pale depths. *Keep calm, keep calm, panic is what kills.* The currents were stronger than he was. But he had a purpose, which they did not. He had the brains to use them. Let them whirl him under – he felt his cheek scraped across a stone – for they would cast him back again and –

Somehow he was by Keshchyi. He was treading water, gulping a lungful when he could, up and down, up and down, away and back, always snatching to untangle those cables around the wing, until after a time beyond time, Keshchyi was loose.

Thuriak extended a hand. Keshchyi took it. Dazed, wounded, plumage soaked, he could not raise himself, nor could Thuriak drag him up alone.

A billow hurled Nat forward. His skull flew at the reef where the boat tossed in shards. Barely soon enough, he touched the controls of his gravbelt and rose.

He grabbed Keshchyi's other arm and switched the power output of his unit to Overload. Between them, he and Thuriak brought their comrade to land.

'My life is yours, Nathaniel Falkayn,' said Keshchyi in the house. 'I beg your leave to honor you.'

'Aye, aye,' whispered through the rustling dimness where the Weathermaker Choth had gathered.

156

'Awww . . . ' Nat mumbled. His cheeks felt hot. He wanted to say, 'Please, all I ask is, don't tell my parents what kind of trouble I got my silly self into.' But that wouldn't be courteous, in this grave ceremony that his friends were holding for him.

It ended at last, however, and he and Thuriak got a chance to slip off by themselves, to the same balcony from which they had started. The short Avalonian day was drawing to a close. Sunbeams lay level across the fields. They shimmered off the sea, beyond which were homes of men. The air was still, and cool, and full of the scent of growing things.

'I have learned much today,' Thuriak said seriously.

'Well, I hope you've learned to be more careful in your next boat,' Nat tried to laugh. *I wish they'd stop making such a fuss about me,* he thought. *They will in time, and we can relax and enjoy each other, Meanwhile, though –*

'I have learned how good it is that strengths be different, so that they may be shared.'

'Well, yes, sure. Wasn't that the whole idea behind this colony?'

And standing there between sky and sea, Nat remembered swimming, diving, surfing, all the years of his life, brightness and laughter of the water that kissed his face and embraced his whole body, the riding on splendid waves and questing into secret twilit depths, the sudden astonishing beauty of a fish or a rippled sandy bottom, sunlight a-dance overhead . . . and he looked at the Ythrian and felt a little sorry for him.

For his last chapter, Hloch returns to A. A. Craig's *Tales of the Great Frontier.* The author was a Terran who traveled widely, gathering material for his historical narratives, during a pause in the Troubles, several lifetimes after the World-Taking. When he visited Avalon, he heard of an incident from the person, then aged, who had experienced it, and made therefrom the story which follows. Though fictionalized, the account is substantially accurate. Though dealing with no large matter, it seems a fitting one wherewith to close.

RESCUE ON AVALON

The Ythrian passed overhead in splendor. Sunlight on feathers made bronze out of his six-meter wingspan and the proudly held golden-eyed head. His crest and tail were white as the snowpeaks around, trimmed with black. He rode the wind like its conqueror.

Against his will, Jack Birnam confessed the sight was beautiful. But it was duty which brought up his binoculars. If the being made a gesture of greeting, he owed his own race the courtesy of a return salute; and Ythrians often forgot that human vision was less keen than theirs. *I have to be especially polite when I'm in country that belongs to them,* the boy thought. Bitterness rushed through him. *And this does, now, it does. Oh, curse our bargaining Parliament!*

Under magnification, he clearly saw the arched carnivore muzzle with its oddly delicate lips; the talons which evolution had made into hands; the claws at the 'elbows' of the wings, which served as feet on the ground; the gill-like slits in the body, bellows pumped by the flight muscles, a biological supercharger making it possible for a creature that size to get aloft. He could even see by the plumage that this was a middle-aged male, and of some importance to judge by the ornate belt, pouch, and dagger which were all that he wore.

Though the Ythrian had undoubtedly noticed Jack, he gave no sign. That was likely just his custom. Choths differed as much in their ways as human nations did, and Jack remembered hearing that the Stormgate folk, who would be moving into these parts, were quite reserved. Nevertheless the boy muttered at him, 'You can call it dignity if you want. I call it snobbery, and I don't like you either.'

The being dwindled until he vanished behind a distant ridge. *He's probably bound for Peace Deep on the far side, to hunt,* Jack decided. *And I wanted to visit there ... Well, why not, anyway? I'll scarcely meet him; won't be going down into the gorge myself. The mountains have room for both of us – for a while, till his people come and settle them.*

He hung the glasses on his packframe and started walking again through loneliness.

The loftiest heights on the planet Avalon belong to the Andromeda Range. But that is a name bestowed by humans. Not for nothing do the Ythrians who have joined them in their colonizing venture call that region the Weathermother. Almost exactly two days – twenty-two hours – after he had spied the stranger, a hurricane caught Jack Birnam. Born and raised here, he was used to sudden tempests. The rapidly spinning globe was always breeding them. Yet the violence of this one astonished him.

He was in no danger. It had not been foolish to set off by himself on a trip into the wilderness. He would have preferred a companion, of course, but none of his friends happened to be free; and he didn't expect he'd ever have

162

another chance to visit the beloved land. He knew it well. He intended merely to hike, not climb. At age twenty-four (or seventeen, if you counted the years of an Earth where he had never been) he was huskier than many full-grown men. In case of serious difficulty, he need merely send a distress signal by his pocket transceiver. Homing on it, an aircar from the nearest rescue station in the foothills should reach him in minutes.

If the sky was fit to fly in!

When wind lifted and clouds whirled like night out of the north, he made his quick preparations. His sleeping bag, with hood and breathing mask for really foul conditions, would keep him warm at lower temperatures than occurred elsewhere on Avalon. Unrolled and erected over it as a kind of pup tent, a sheet of duraplast would stop hailstones or blown débris. The collapsible alloy frame, light but equally sturdy, he secured to four pegs whose explosive heads had driven them immovably into bedrock. This shelter wasn't going anywhere. When he had brought himself and his equipment inside, he had nothing to do but wait out the several shrieking hours which followed.

Nonetheless, he was almost frightened at the fury, and half-stunned by the time it died away.

Crawling forth, he found the sun long set. Morgana, the moon, was full, so radiant that it crowded most stars out of view. Remote snowfields glittered against blue-black heaven; boulders and shrubs on the ridgetop where Jack was camped shone as if turned to silver, while a nearby stream flowed like mercury. The cluck and chuckle of water, the boom of a more distant cataract, were the only sounds. After the wind-howl, this stillness felt almost holy. The air was chill but carried odors of plant life, sharp trefoil, sweet livewell, and janie. Breath smoked ghostly.

After his long lying motionless, he couldn't sleep. He decided to make a fire, cook a snack and coffee, watch dawn when it came. Here above timberline, the low, tough vegetation wasn't much damaged. But he was sure to find plenty of broken-off wood. The trees below must have suffered far worse. He'd see in the morning. At present, to him those depths were one darkness, hoar-frosted by moonlight.

His transceiver beeped. He stiffened. That meant a general broadcast on the emergency band. Drawing the flat object from his coverall, he flipped its switch for two-way. A human voice lifted small: – 'Mount Farview area. Andromeda Rescue Station Four calling anyone in the Mount Farview area. Andromeda –'

Jack brought the instrument to his mouth. 'Responding,' he said. Inside his quilted garment, he shivered with more than cold. 'John Birnam responding to ARS Four. I . . . I'm a single party, on foot, but if I can help –'

The man at the other end barked: 'Where are you, exactly?'

'It doesn't have a name on the map,' Jack replied, 'but I'm on the south rim of a big canyon which starts about twenty kilometers east-north-east of Farview's top. I'm roughly above the middle of the gorge, that'd be, uh, say thirty kilometers further east.'

It does have a name, though, went through his mind. *I named it Peace Deep, five years ago when I first came on it, because the forest down there is so tall and quiet. Wonder what the Ythrians will call it, after I can't come here anymore?*

'Got you,' answered the man. He must have an aerial survey chart before him. 'John Birnam, you said? I'm Ivar Holm. Did you come through the storm all right?'

'Yes, thanks, I was well prepared. Are you checking?'

'In a way.' Holm spoke grimly. 'Look, this whole

sector's in bad trouble. The prediction on that devil-wind was totally inadequate, a gross underestimate. Not enough meteorological monitors yet, I suppose. Or maybe the colonies are too young to've learned every trick that Avalon can play. Anyhow, things are torn apart down here in the hills – farms, villages, isolated camps – aircars smashed or crashed, including several that belonged to this corps. In spite of help being rushed in from outside, we'll be days in finding and saving the survivors. Our pilots and medics are going to have to forget there ever was such a thing as sleep.'

'I . . . I'm sorry,' Jack said lamely.

'I was praying someone would be in your vicinity. You see, an Ythrian appears to have come to grief thereabouts.'

'An Ythrian!' Jack whispered.

'Not just any Ythrian, either. Ayan, the Wyvan of Stormgate.'

'What?'

'Don't you know about that?' It was very possible. Thus far, the two races hadn't overlapped a great deal. Within the territories they claimed, they had been too busy adapting themselves and their ways to a world that was strange to them both. Jack, whose family were sea ranchers, dwelling on the coast five hundred kilometers westward, had seldom encountered one of the other species. Even a well-educated person might be forgiven for a certain vagueness about details of an entire set of alien societies.

'In the Stormgate choth,' Holm said, ' "Wyvan" comes as close to meaning "Chief" or "President" as you can get in their language. And Stormgate, needing more room as its population grows, had lately acquired this whole part of the Andromedas.'

'I know,' Jack couldn't help blurting in a refreshed

rage. 'The Parliament of Man and the Great Khruath of the Ythrians made their nice little deal, and never mind those of us who spent all the time we could up here because we love the country!'

'Huh? What're you talking about? It was a fair exchange. They turned over some mighty good prairie to us. We don't live by hunting and ranching the way they do. We can't use alps for anything except recreation – and not many of us ever did – and why are you and I wasting time, Birnam?'

Jack set his teeth. 'Go on, please.'

'Well. Ayan went to scout the new land personally, alone. That's Ythrian style. You must be aware what a territorial instinct their race has got. Now I've received a worried call from Stormgate headquarters. His family says he'd have radioed immediately after the blow, if he could, and asked us to relay a message that he wasn't hurt. But he hasn't. Nor did he ever give notice of precisely where he'd be, and no Ythrian on an outing uses enough gear to be readily spotted from the air.'

'A low-power sender won't work out of that particular forest,' Jack said. 'Too much ironleaf growing there.'

'Sunblaze!' Holm groaned. 'Things never do go wrong one at a time, do they?' He drew breath. 'Ordinarily we'd have a fleet of cars out searching, regardless of the difficulty. We can't spare them now, especially since he may well be dead. Nevertheless – You spoke as if you had a clue to his whereabouts.'

Jack paused before answering slowly, 'Yes, I believe I do.'

'What? Quick, for mercy's sake!'

'An Ythrian flew by me a couple of days ago, headed the same way I was. Must've been him. Then when I arrived on this height, down in the canyon I saw smoke rising above the treetops. Doubtless a fire of his. I suppose he'd been hunting and – Well, I didn't pay close attention, but I could point the site out approximately. Why not send a team to where I am?'

Holm kept silent a while. The moonlight seemed to grow more cold and white.

'Weren't you listening, Birnam?' he said at last. 'We need every man and every vehicle we can get, every minute they can be in action. According to my map, that gorge is heavily wooded. Do you mean we should tie up two or three men and a car for hours or days, searching for the exact place – when the chances of him being alive look poor, and . . . you're right on the scene?

'Can't you locate him? Find what the situation is, do what you can to help, and call back with precise information. Given that, we can snake him right out of there, without first wasting man-hours that should go to hundreds of people we know we can save. How about it?'

Now Jack had no voice.

'Hello?' Holm's cry was tiny in the night. 'Hello?'

Jack gripped the transceiver till his knuckles stood bloodless. 'I'm not sure what I can manage,' he said.

'How d'you mean?'

'I'm allergic to Ythrians.'

'*Huh?*'

'Something about their feathers or – It's gotten extremely bad in the last year or two. If I come near one, soon I can hardly breathe. And I didn't bring my antiallergen, this trip. Never expected to need it.'

'Your condition ought to be curable.'

'The doctor says it is, but that requires facilities we don't have on Avalon. RNA transformation, you know. My family can't afford to send me to a more developed planet. I just avoid those creatures.'

'You can at least go look, can't you?' Holm pleaded. 'I appreciate the risk, but if you're extra careful – '

'Oh, yes,' Jack said reluctantly. 'I can do that.'

With the starkness of his folk, Ayan had shut his mind to pain while he waited for rescue or death. From time to time he shrilled forth hunting calls, and these guided Jack to him after the boy reached the general location. They had grown steadily weaker, though.

Far down a steep slope, the Ythrian sprawled rather than lay, resting against a chasuble bush. Everywhere around him were ripped branches and fallen boles, a tangle which had made it a whole day's struggle for Jack to get here. Sky, fading toward sunset, showed through rents in the canopy overhead. Mingled with green and gold of other trees was the shimmering, glittering purple foliage of ironleaf.

The alatan bone in Ayan's left wing was bent at an ugly angle. That fracture made it alike impossible for him to fly or walk. Gaunt, exhausted, he still brought his crest erect as the human blundered into view. Hoarseness thickened the accent of his Anglic speech: 'Welcome indeed!'

Jack stopped three meters off, panting, sweating despite the chill, knees wobbly beneath him. He knew it was idiotic, but could think of nothing else than: 'How ... are you, ... sir?' *And why call him 'sir,' this land-robber?*

'In poor case,' dragged out of Ayan's throat. 'Well it is that you arrived. I would not have lasted a second night. The wind cast a heavy bough against my wing and broke it. My rations and equipment were scattered; I do not think you could find them yourself.' The three fingers and two thumbs of a hand gestured at the transceiver clipped on his belt. 'Somehow this must also have been disabled. My calls for help have drawn no response.'

'They wouldn't, here.' Jack pointed to the sinister love-liness which flickered in a breeze above. 'Didn't you know? That's called ironleaf. It draws the metal from the soil and concentrates pure particles, to attract pollinating bugs by the shininess. Absorbs radio waves. Nobody should go into an area like this without a partner.'

'I was unaware – even as the weather itself caught me by surprise. The territory is foreign to me.'

'It's home country to *me*.' Fists clenched till nails bit into palms.

Ayan's stare sharpened upon Jack. Abruptly he realized how peculiar his behavior must seem. The Ythrian needed help, and the human only stood there. Jack couldn't simply leave him untended; he would die.

The boy braced himself and said in a hurry: 'Listen. Listen good, because maybe I won't be able to repeat this. I'll have to scramble back up to where I can transmit. Then they'll send a car that I can guide to you. But I can't go till morning. I'd lose my way, or break my neck, groping in the dark through this wreckage the storm's made. First I'll do what's necessary for you. We better plan every move in advance.'

'Why?' asked Ayan quietly.

'Because you make me sick! I mean – allergy – I'm going to get asthma and hives, working on you. Unless we minimize my exposure, I may be too ill to travel tomorrow.'

'I see.' For all his resentment, Jack was awed by the self-control. 'Do you perchance carry anagon in your first-aid kit? No? Pity. I believe that is the sole painkiller which works on both our species. *Hrau.* You can toss me your filled canteen and some food immediately. I am near collapse from both thirst and hunger.'

'It's human-type stuff, you realize,' Jack warned. While men and Ythrians could eat many of the same things, each diet lacked certain essentials of the other. For that matter, native Avalonian life did not hold adequate nutrition for either colonizing race. The need to maintain separate ecologies was a major reason why they tended to live apart. *I can't ever return*, Jack thought. *Even if the new dwellers allowed me to visit, my own body wouldn't.*

'Calories, at least,' Ayan reminded him. 'Though I have feathers to keep me warmer than your skin would, last night burned most of what energy I had left.'

Jack obliged. 'Next,' he proposed, 'I'll start a fire and cut enough wood to last you till morning.'

Was Ayan startled? That alien face wasn't readable. It looked as if the Ythrian was about to say something and then changed his mind. The boy went on: 'What sort of preliminary care do you yourself need?'

'Considerable, I fear,' said Ayan. Jack's heart sank. 'Infection is setting in, and I doubt you carry an antibiotic safe for use on me; so my injuries must be thoroughly cleansed. The bone must be set and splinted, however roughly. Otherwise – I do not wish to complain, but the pain at every slightest movement is becoming quite literally unendurable. I barely managed to keep the good wing flapping, thus myself halfway warm, last night. Without support for the broken one, I could not stay conscious to tend the fire.'

Jack forgot that he hated this being. 'Oh, gosh, no! I wasn't thinking straight. You take my bag. I can, uh, sort of fold you into it.'

'Let us see. Best we continue planning and preparations.'

Jack nodded jerkily. The time soon came when he must take a breath, hold it as long as possible, and go to the Ythrian.

It was worse than his worst imagining.

At the end, he lay half-strangled, eyes puffed nearly shut, skin one great burning and itch, wheezed, wept, and

170

shuddered. Crouched near the blaze, Ayan looked at him across the meters of cold, thickening dusk which again separated them. He barely heard the nonhuman voice:

'You need that bedroll more than I do, especially so when you must have strength back by dawn to make the return trip. Take your rest.'

Jack crept to obey. He was too wretched to realize what the past hour must have been like for Ayan.

First light stole bleak between trees. The boy wakened to a ragged call: '*Khrraah, khrraah, khrraah*, human – ' For a long while, it seemed, he fought his way through mists and cobwebs. Suddenly, with a gasp, he came to full awareness.

The icy air went into his lungs through a throat much less swollen than before. Bleariness and ache still possessed his head, but he could think, he could see . . .

Ayan lay by the ashes of the fire. He had raised himself on his hands to croak aloud. His crest drooped, his eyes were glazed. '*Khrraah* – '

Jack writhed from his bag and stumbled to his feet. 'What happened?' he cried in horror.

'I . . . fainted . . . only recovered this moment – Pain, weariness, and . . . lack of nourishment – I feared I might collapse but hoped I would not – '

It stabbed through Jack: *Why didn't I stop to think? Night before last, pumping that wing – the biological supercharger kindling his metabolism beyond anything a human can experience – burning not just what fuel his body had left, but vitamins that weren't in the rations I could give him –*

'Why didn't you insist on the bedding?' the human cried in anguish of his own. 'I could've stayed awake all right!'

'I was not certain you could,' said the harsh whisper.

'You appeared terribly ill, and . . . it would have been wrong, that the young die for the old . . . I know too little about your kind – ' The Ythrian crumpled.

'And I about yours.' Jack sped to him, took him in his arms, brought him to the warm bag and tucked him in with enormous care. Presently Ayan's eyes fluttered open, and Jack could feed him.

The asthma and eruptions weren't nearly as bad as earlier. Jack hardly noticed, anyway. When he had made sure Ayan was resting comfortably, supplies in easy reach, he himself gulped a bite to eat and started off.

It would be a stiff fight, in his miserable shape, to get past the ironleaf before dark. He'd do it, though. He knew he would.

The doctors kept him one day in the hospital. Recovered, he borrowed protective garments and a respirator, and went to the Ythrian ward to say goodbye.

Ayan lay in one of the frames designed for his race. He was alone in his room. Its window stood open to a lawn and tall trees – Avalonian king's-crown, Ythrian windnest, Earthly oak – and a distant view of snowpeaks. Light spilled from heaven. The air sang. Ayan looked wistfully outward.

But he turned his head and, yes, smiled as Jack entered, recognizing him no matter how muffled up he was. 'Greeting, galemate,' he said.

The boy had spent his own time abed studying usages of Stormgate. He flushed; for he could have been called nothing more tender and honoring than 'galemate.'

'How are you?' he inquired awkwardly.

'I shall get well, because of you.' Ayan grew grave. 'Jack,' he murmured, 'can you come near me?'

'Sure, as long's I'm wearing this.' The human approached. Talons reached out to clasp his gloved hand.

'I have been talking with Ivar Holm and others,' Ayan said very low. 'You resent me, my whole people, do you not?'

'Aw, well – '

'I understand. We were taking from you a place you hold dear. Jack, you, and any guests of yours, will forever be welcome there, to roam as you choose. Indeed, the time is over-past for our two kinds to intermingle freely.'

'But . . . I mean, thank you, sir,' Jack stammered, 'but I can't.'

'Your weakness? Yes-s-s.' Ayan uttered the musical Ythrian equivalent of a chuckle. 'I suspect it is of largely psychosomatic origin, and might fade of itself when your anger does. But naturally, my choth will send you off-planet for a complete cure.'

Jack could only stare and stutter.

Ayan lifted his free hand. 'Thank us not. We need the closeness of persons like you, who would not abandon even an enemy.'

'But you aren't!' burst from Jack. 'I'll be proud to call you my friend!'

To those who have traveled with him this far, Hloch gives thanks. It is his hope that he has aided you to a little deeper sight, and thereby done what honor he was able to his choth and to the memory of his mother, Rennhi the wise.

Countless are the currents which streamed together at Avalon. Here we have flown upon only a few. Of these, some might well have been better chosen. Yet it seems to Hloch that all, in one way or another, raise a little higher than erstwhile his knowledge of that race with which ours is to share this world until God the Hunter descends upon both. May this be true for you as well, O people.

Now *The Earth Book of Stormgate* is ended. From my tower I see the great white sweep of the snows upon Mount Anrovil. I feel the air blow in and caress my feathers. Yonder sky is calling. I will go.

Fair winds forever.

NEL BESTSELLERS

T037061	BLOOD AND MONEY	*Thomas Thompson*	£1.50
T045692	THE BLACK HOLE	*Alan Dean Foster*	95p
T049817	MEMORIES OF ANOTHER DAY	*Harold Robbins*	£1.95
T049701	THE DARK	*James Herbert*	£1.50
T045773	CLAIR RAYNER'S LIFEGUARD		£2.50
T045528	THE STAND	*Stephen King*	£1.75
T065475	I BOUGHT A MOUNTAIN	*Thomas Firbank*	£1.50
T050203	IN THE TEETH OF THE EVIDENCE	*Dorothy L. Sayers*	£1.25
T050777	STRANGER IN A STRANGE LAND	*Robert Heinlein*	£1.75
T050807	79 PARK AVENUE	*Harold Robbins*	£1.75
T042308	DUNE	*Frank Herbert*	£1.50
T045137	THE MOON IS A HARSH MISTRESS	*Robert Heinlein*	£1.25
T050149	THE INHERITORS	*Harold Robbins*	£1.75
T049620	RICH MAN, POOR MAN	*Irwin Shaw*	£1.60
T046710	EDGE 36: TOWN ON TRIAL	*George G. Gilman*	£1.00
T037541	DEVIL'S GUARD	*Robert Elford*	£1.25
T050629	THE RATS	*James Herbert*	£1.25
T050874	CARRIE	*Stephen King*	£1.50
T050610	THE FOG	*James Herbert*	£1.25
T041867	THE MIXED BLESSING	*Helen Van Slyke*	£1.50
T038629	THIN AIR	*Simpson & Burger*	95p
T038602	THE APOCALYPSE	*Jeffrey Konvitz*	95p
T046850	WEB OF EVERYWHERE	*John Brunner*	85p

NEL P.O. BOX 11, FALMOUTH TR10 9EN, CORNWALL

Postage charge:

U.K. Customers. Please allow 40p for the first book, 18p for the second book, 13p for each additional book ordered, to a maximum charge of £1.49, in addition to cover price.

B.F.P.O. & Eire. Please allow 40p for the first book, 18p for the second book, 13p per copy for the next 7 books, thereafter 7p per book, in addition to cover price.

Overseas Customers. Please allow 60p for the first book plus 18p per copy for each additional book, in addition to cover price.

Please send cheque or postal order (no currency).

Name ....

Address ....

....

Title ....

While every effort is made to keep prices steady, it is sometimes necessary to increase prices at short notice. New English Library reserve the right to show on covers and charge new retail prices which may differ from those advertised in the text or elsewhere.(5)